BOWERY GIRL

KIM TAYLOR BLAKEMORE

KINGFISHER PRESS
www.kingfisherpress.us

Paperback ISBN: 978-0-9905843-0-8
eISBN: 978-0-9905843-1-5

First published in 2006 by Viking, a division of Penguin

CREDITS:
Editor: Sharyn November
Cover Design: Indie Designz

February 1883

RELEASE

DOWN THE STREET STRODE a young woman, who could have been anywhere between thirteen and twenty. She didn't know her own age, so she had decided on sixteen. She was not pretty, nor was she plain. Her hair was brown, not dirty and not clean, and she kept it in a loose bun. Her eyebrows were dark and full, and from beneath them, her winter-gray eyes missed nothing. A matchstick hung from the corner of her mouth, and every so often she shifted it to the other side, then back again to its original spot. She had been told by several do-gooders at several charity houses that this was a reprehensible habit, which was why she never stopped doing it.

Her dress was neither this year's fashion nor the last; it was patched in places, and frayed along the bottom. The material was coarse brown cotton, solid and indifferent. With each step, the young woman, whose name was Mollie Flynn, admired the black sheen of her new boots. Mollie was quite proud of them. She'd pinched them a week earlier from Friedrich's Secondhand Shop on Chambers Street. They were bright as black could be, and she polished them every night to keep them so.

An Elevated train rattled above, drowning out the rat-a-tat from the shooting gallery, the shouts of drivers as they jockeyed their carts and horses for a bit of space, the competing songs of violins and out-of-tune pianos floating from saloon doorways.

She walked by an old woman in an alcove, selling buttons she'd probably picked out of trash bins. Another woman trundled slowly past, a huge pile of fabric balanced on her head. Two boys played hoops and sticks, laughing and shouting to each other. The boys' laughter, the woman's determined footfall, the call to buy buttons, the wheedling song of pullers-in trying to tempt passersby into the billiard room, the dancehall, the used-jewelry store, the pawnshop—the rhythm made Mollie dizzy.

At Maud Riley's vegetable stand, a tall man bargained over a rather measly cabbage. He nodded, a deal struck, then fumbled in the inside pocket of his coat for his wallet. Maud wrapped two cabbages and a few potatoes in newspaper and pulled a bit of twine tight.

Mollie sucked a bit on her matchstick and narrowed her eyes. She wasn't looking at Maud Riley's slaughter of a poor cabbage. She was watching the man's wallet, which flapped open, hung about, and generally looked like it was going to jump right out of his incompetent fingers.

Now that, Mollie thought, would be the easiest wallet to pinch in the world. It would only take a second. Her fingers tingled with possibility.

But she was late already. And she had a pocket full of coins, enough at least for a good meal of oysters and beer. For it was time—finally and after so many months!—to collect Annabelle Lee from the steps of the criminal courts, which everyone in New York City called "The Tombs." The sky above was blue and heavenly, so sharp and new with the beginning of spring that she thought she could single out each crystal that made it.

Mollie bought a hot wine and a bag of chestnuts from a pushcart on the corner of Centre and Worth. "What time ya got?" she asked the cart's owner.

"One."

"One?" She gulped down the wine and set the cup on the pushcart. She peered into the shadows of the thick, dark granite columns of the prison. There were so many people going in and out, so much shouting. Here was a fellow coming out and hugging his wife. And there was a drunk being dragged by a copper up the steps.

A milk cart rolled by, and then a delivery van, and damn if the trolley didn't block her! She'd best cross over, so Annabelle could find her. She darted across the street, careful to hop over the tracks that coursed the middle of Centre Street—no need to bring bad luck on such a day.

She passed the wrought-iron fence that guarded two scrawny winter-dead trees and a narrow patch of soil and stopped directly at the bottom of the gray steps.

In November, Annabelle Lee had been caught with her hand in a detective's pocket. Though he was quite happy with the service she had provided him, he was not happy to then be robbed. She had been sent to Blackwell's Island, and it was noted by the fat judge that she was "incurably saucy and a menace to society."

Mollie missed Annabelle Lee. It was Annabelle Lee who had held out her hand, had pulled Mollie from the rags she had crawled under to warm herself. Annabelle had walked the streets even then, a twelve-year-old porcelain doll-child. She worked the corner next to the Ragpickers' Lot. She'd left Mollie bread and beer, like you'd leave scraps and fish bones for a feral cat you wanted to tame. It was Annabelle Lee who had given her the name Mollie Flynn.

They had lived together in a cellar that ran underneath Batavia between Roosevelt and Chambers, just around the corner from where they lived now, close by the brewery, where men gave them free drinks just for a chance to grab at Annabelle's girlish breasts. Annabelle never let them grab at Mollie's.

Mollie missed the strolls in the streets during the dead times, those times between the lunch crowd and the evening drunk crowd. Annabelle used to laugh for no reason—they both laughed for no reason. Sometimes they'd sneak into the Thalia Theatre and watch rehearsals. Other times, they'd walk the East River docks, wondering where each ship was headed—Bombay, Barcelona, Cape Town, Buenos Aires. Annabelle said her father's father had been a deckhand on a slave ship, and he had shown her the shackles once to prove it.

On Sundays, when good Irish Catholics went to Mass, Annabelle and Mollie would visit the psychic who lodged on the first floor of a Batavia Street tenement. Annabelle dressed plainly in gray, though insisted on wearing her wig, for she loved the way the blonde curls bounced around her face as she walked.

The psychic's name was Hermione Montreal. She was old; the paint she put on her lips bled into the lines all around her mouth. She always told them, in a croaky voice, that they were destined for greatness and would marry well. Each

Sunday they came back and told her that neither event had happened and they wanted their money back. But she served them whiskey and cookies and told them the stars never lied.

Now, in front of the Tombs, Mollie thought she might spot Annabelle from her blonde curls, but then realized that the wig hung on the wall at home; Annabelle's own hair was dark as half the throng.

And then she laughed out loud, for of course it would be easy to find Annabelle Lee! Why, there she was, parading down the hard steps, red leather shoes peeping and teasing from under her skirts.

"You're here." Annabelle smiled.

"And I'm early, so what ya got to say about that?"

Annabelle put a hand on her hip and pretended to fluff her hair with the other. "Do you like the outfit? Courtesy of the good Ladies of Charity. Gave me a Bible, too, but it somehow got lost. Tried to take my shoes, but I said I'd claw their eyes out and bite their ears."

Mollie took her in. She wasn't at all the Annabelle who'd gone to Blackwell's Island four months ago. Her skin was pale, almost purple around her brown eyes. And Lord, the clothes she wore were of the roughest material, like sacks, not even the hint of a bustle or corseted waist.

"Was it horrible?" Mollie asked.

"Why, no, oysters and beer and twenty servants to dress you."

"How grand."

"No. Not really." Annabelle slung her arm through Mollie's and pulled her down the street. "Look at that sky. What a goddamn blue sky. On Blackwell's it was once around the yard, even if you wanted more."

Blackwell's Island sat opposite Sixty-First Street, out in

the East River—a small island ringed with pretty green trees. Trees meant to hide all the darkness that sat at its center. A person went to Blackwell's for one of three reasons: for penance, for insanity, or for death. It was home to the thief, the beggar, the consumptive, the lunatic, the very old and very poor, the incorrigible, the wanton, the depraved, the unlucky. Superintendents, wardens, and turnkeys watched their wretched guests with cruel eyes. Should a new mother throw a fit over the rotten state of the proffered food, her baby was torn from her and sent to another family in the Far West. Should an old woman find herself a widow without any recourse to pay her rent, off she was shipped to the Island, to work at braiding straw until her fingers bled. If a man wandered the wrong street, a "kind" policemen might dislike his look and charge him with vagrancy, and then it was through the court at the Tombs and on to Blackwell's to be made a "better man." A third or fourth time at the workhouse—well, then, the penitentiary was deemed your next abode. And life became three square meals of bread and water, striped clothing, and your own cell locked tight at night.

"What'd you do while I was gone?" Annabelle asked.

"Seamus took me to see Annie Hindle do her male impersonation over at Tony Pastor's club. She sure is a handsome man, what she's a woman and all."

"I hear her husband's really a girl."

"Do ya?"

"Picked some full pockets?"

"It's been cold. Did a few sneak thieves for the boys, though, into some liquor warehouses."

"Let me see your fingers." Annabelle took Mollie's hand and turned it back and forth. "Ooh, nice and soft. Keeping up with the butter?"

"When I can afford it."

"Good girl. Can't be a pickpocket without nice hands." She kissed Mollie's palm, then let go. "Thought maybe Tommy might have come."

"He's meeting us tonight at Lefty's."

Annabelle's lips went tight, and then she laughed sharp as a knife. "Shoulda known it'd be you and not him."

"I kept the place for us," Mollie said. She did not say that she'd borrowed the rent money from Tommy, for the winter had been bitter and the racket was frozen as the sky. She did not say her hands weren't as fast as they'd been before, and that sometimes the cold burned them stiff.

"You always take care of me, don't you?"

"I owe you."

Annabelle touched Mollie's cheek. "You don't owe me nothing. Except for your ever-loving life."

Mollie looked closer at her friend. Annabelle had always been thin, for she knew the best johns on the streets were those looking for some bit of a virgin to conquer. But now, there was a weight to her cheeks and a heaviness to her walk.

"I want to get cleaned up," Annabelle said. "I want a bath. You didn't sell my clothes, did you?"

"Course not. I kept them hanging on the wall, so's the rats wouldn't eat them."

"Good, then. A change of clothes, then a bath." Annabelle frowned. And although she kept pace with Mollie, her attention seemed to be both inward and then outward, struggling with a disappointment that Mollie had seen many times before. "He got a new girl?"

"Annabelle..."

"Course he does, doesn't he?"

The tenement at 32 Oak Street was squeezed between two others, and the alley entrance was blocked by boxes of empty liquor bottles. Mollie and Annabelle stayed close together as they made their way through the narrow corridor. They kept their eyes to the ground, for one wrong step would land shoes in offal or garbage. The air held the familiar scent of home: cabbage, potatoes, and rot. Wet laundry hung overhead, untouched by any breeze. They crossed the yard that separated the front tenement from the back rookery, holding their breath against the stench of the outhouses. Mollie pulled hard at the rookery's swollen front door—one time, two times, three—until the door scraped against the landing and swung free.

A single gaslight, bare of globe or cage, brightened the first three steps; beyond was darkness.

"Remember the way?" Mollie asked.

"How could I forget?"

They lifted their skirts and ascended.

Annabelle stopped at the trough on the second floor and splashed her face with water that dripped from a spigot on the wall. The squawk of a violin came from one of the flats. A pot clattered behind another door. "Give me a second to rest." She leaned against the wall, and even in the murky light, Mollie saw how hard it was for Annabelle to catch her breath. "Jesus, you think we'd know not to get a place on the fifth floor. At least they could put in railings, so when my legs give out I can pull myself up."

"Ah, you're just not used to it now," Mollie said. "Give yourself a day and you'll be running up here with your eyes closed."

"Eyes open or closed, it's still dark, ain't it?" She took Mollie's hand.

"Got some Italians next door now. Sew buttons. Two kids and God knows how many adults. They stink, that's all I know. Put garlic in everything and don't never take baths. Seamus says they're gonna ruin this neighborhood."

Annabelle blew out a breath. "Think we might find a place on the first floor when leases come up in May?"

"My, how upper-class that'll make us." Mollie pulled out the key she wore around her neck and let them in. She crossed the room to the barrel that served as their table and lit the candle, then pulled a shard of coal from a bucket and pushed it in the cast-iron stove. She lifted a jar from the shelf near the coal stove, scooped a bit of tea into a pot, then picked up a pail of water, pouring enough for two cups.

"You hung my clothes." Annabelle ran her fingers over the fabrics of her dresses. Even in the dim light, the blues and pinks and reds danced. "I'll have to let these out a bit. No corset, I guess."

"I even repapered the walls. Got a grand serial going on. I'll read ya later."

Annabelle lifted her wig from a hook, pulled it on, and flipped at the fake curls to make them bob. Then she bent to the piece of mirror on a shelf in the corner, and adjusted the wig's placement.

"Aw, *now* I recognize you," Mollie said.

"Do you?" Annabelle pinched her cheeks. "Where's my rouge?"

"In the box under the bed. I'll get it."

Annabelle twisted the lid open and dabbed the red on her cheeks and lips. "Want some?" She held out the jar.

"Nah."

"Natural beauty you got, Mollie." She opened a small box that held blue powder and a tiny brush, and then ran the color over her lids. "Better, huh?" Annabelle reached to her three dresses. "Now, which color for Tommy? He likes the red, I think."

"Ya look better in blue."

Annabelle pulled the red from the hook and shook it out.

She held it to her waist, sighed, and sat heavily on the edge of the bed they shared. "God, open a window. Oh, I forget, we don't have one." She turned the dress inside out. "I can take some fabric from round the bustle, here, and drape it in front. Make my own style. Give me your knife, Mollie."

As Annabelle tore at the seams of her dress, Mollie pulled the chair from the wall and sat, crossing her legs. She stuck a matchstick in her mouth and leaned back, so the front chair legs lifted from the floor. This was right; this was like it always was, Annabelle making pretty things and Mollie sitting and watching. The light from the candle spread in a golden circle.

Annabelle glanced up from her work. "Tell me about your world."

"My world?"

"Your world without me."

"Oh, that. I became a Protestant. Go to church every day. Bought a horse and carriage to tour the park." Mollie shook her head in mock sadness. "Being rich is so boring, really."

"The day I see you in any church, Mollie Flynn, is the day I'll dance naked at Lefty's and give all the money thrown at me to charity. Ow. Haven't done any sewing in a while." Annabelle shook her thumb, then sucked the blood from the tip. "How's Seamus?"

"Same as ever. Wanting more than ever. What the hell. I ain't marrying him." She stood, and moved two chipped cups from the shelf to the barrel. Using her skirt as a towel, she picked up the pot and poured the tea. "I mean what the hell, ya know? What does he think?"

Someone pounded against the wall. Mollie grabbed for the mirror so it wouldn't fall. Then she kicked at the wall.

"Shut up, ya filthy"—she kicked the wall again—"stinkin' Wops!"

More pounding. Annabelle's dresses fluttered with each hit.

Mollie whirled to Annabelle. "Was I yelling? I don't think I was yelling." She made a fist and thumped twice, tearing the newspaper that lined the walls. "I wasn't yelling, ya sons of bitches!"

Annabelle laughed. She set the needle she worked with on the barrel's top, and wiped her eyes. "Aw, ya daft bitch. I'm so glad to be home."

A BATH

THEY WERE ASKED TO write their names in the ledger at the East Side Baths. The large, wafer-thin pages were filled with the names and dates of all the visitors who had entered; upon the approval and signature of the head matron, five cents were to be deposited in a coffee tin.

The building had once been a mansion, and its back gardens had stretched to the banks of the East River. The elegance could still be seen in the welcoming curves of the banister railing, the colored glass above the door where Jesus' lamb lay in green meadows, in the high ceilings carved with angels and bouquets of flowers. Where had the family fled who had once lived here, in the time of Madison and Adams? To Washington Square, perhaps, or farther away—the Forties off Fifth Avenue. They fled the immigrant masses: the Irish and Germans who came through the gates of Castle Garden and invaded the East Side. The fathers and sons of the old families had continued to conduct their business here, although they were careful to place large signs in the windows of their shops and factories stating NO DOGS OR IRISH ALLOWED.

But that was before. Now, the Irish were, if not respectable, at least established in their rough-and-tumble strong-hold. And as the good American families had done to them, so the Irish did to the newcomers who now flowed through Castle Garden.

The head matron scowled at Mollie. She crossed her ample arms and narrowed her eyes. Her jowls were gray as the dirt in the corners of the entryway. She waited for Mollie's name.

Mollie dipped the pen in the ink bottle.

The light from the stained-glass meadow above her suffused the room with a green phosphorescent tint. Mollie held the pen aloft; the black ink slid in one large drop to the very tip, where it ballooned and then dropped to the paper below.

"Now look what you've done! I won't be able to read three names now, you stupid girl. I'm meant to transfer the names from this ledger to Miss DuPre's ledger, and you have ruined it."

"What are you keeping the names for?" Annabelle asked.

"I ought to take your five cents just for defiling my ledger. And you've held up the line—look." The matron pointed to the doorway.

She was right: Young girls, women holding babies close to their bosoms, cheap shawls, no shawls, thin shoes, thin hair, children with bowed legs certainly caused by rickets, stood in a long line behind Mollie.

"Now sign your name."

Mollie's hand dropped to the empty line, 152. In her very best handwriting, she signed, *Dolley Madison*.

The head matron plucked the pen from her hand and pointed it at Annabelle. "Come, come, come."

"She can't write," Mollie said. "I'll sign for her." She took back the pen and filled line 153: *Martha Washington.*

The head matron turned the heavy ledger to face her. She attacked the page with her pen, marking her initials boldly. She cocked her head at the ping of Mollie's coins in the coffee tin. "Take a towel from the basket to the right of the door, then up the stairs. Take any tub that's empty, and if there isn't an empty one, share with another girl. The faucet's on the wall—the under matron will add one kettle of hot water—scrub, then wipe, then redress. Ten minutes."

Mollie and Annabelle barely heard her. They darted for the stairs, grabbing a towel.

"Since when's there a sign-in?" Annabelle asked.

"Since some rich bitch bought this building and the one next door. Got classrooms and everything over there. Wait till you see her. Harps on and on about us improving our lives. Can't take a bath in peace anymore."

Mollie smelled the clean sting of soap before she entered the long room. Girls giggled. Water sloshed against iron tubs and dribbled from faucets.

"Where's all the tubs?" Mollie counted only ten, where there had been twenty. Plugged pipes extended from one wall; the only evidence of the missing tubs were dark rectangular water stains.

"You'll have to ask Miss DuPre that." The under matron who answered made a disapproving sound from between the gap in her teeth. "Five went to the basement and one up the stairs to you-know-who's new rooms. Knows what to do with the tubs, she does, but not what to do with us. Isn't that right, Peggy?"

Another under matron swayed by, her hands gripping a pot of steaming water. Her gray hair, sizzled and steamed all the day, stuck out in tiny erratic curlicues. "Serving the poor and never a care for the ones of us who make an honest living."

"*Made* an honest living."

"Some's luckier than us. Head matron downstairs is to remain head matron of the what's it called? *Settlement house.*" Peggy slopped the hot water into an empty tub. She let the bucket clatter to the floor, then twisted open the faucet. Water gushed, brown with minerals and rust, into the tub. "Not much else you can expect of one of *them*, is it? Not an ounce of kindness and not a bit of respect for the pope." She crossed herself and rolled her eyes. The faucet squealed against its metal as she shut the tap. "Well, get in, girls, you only got the few minutes."

Mollie glanced at Annabelle. "Looks like we're sharing."

Gray scum floated on the water; Mollie hoped it was only from the last girl's soap. She put her hand in the water, and then pulled away sharply. Oh, how cold it was! How would she ever sit in the bath itself?

There were two pegs on the wall on either side of the tub: for clothes and for towels. Combs hung from ropes (so as not to be "mistakenly" taken). Large blocks of soap sat on shelves. Across the room, kettles bubbled atop heavy cast-iron stoves.

The under matrons sat near the stoves, each woman dressed in the cheap rags of the tenement, each serious about her job, which was to keep order.

But how to keep down the squeals of glee and the screams as the girls first touched the cool water? Or the laughter from the mothers, happy to have left their baby or toddler in another room, to have even these few precious moments free from family responsibility? No matter how loudly the under matrons barked and shushed, it proved impossible to quiet all the temperaments in the room. The under matrons kept strict time over their tubs, if not the noise level; they knew to the second who should get out to let another "poor girl" in.

Annabelle and Mollie undressed, hanging up their skirts and shirts and underthings.

"Damn, that water looks cold as a witch's tit," Annabelle said.

Holding her breath, Mollie flung herself into the tub. "Ain't so bad."

Annabelle removed her wig, careful to hang it so it would not fall onto the wet floor. She hugged her arms to her chest and dipped a toe in the water.

Mollie blinked once, then again. "Jesus Christ, Annabelle. You're pregnant."

"Looks like it." She climbed in, facing Mollie. She held her breath and submerged her face. Bubbles wisped across the water. Then she sat up abruptly, sloshing water over the edge. "I tried to get rid of it, got some herbs, but they only sent me to the infirmary for a coupla days."

"Shit."

"That's all you can say?"

"What the hell else can I say?" Mollie grabbed the edge of her towel, wet it, and rubbed it into the large soap block.

Oh, how the grime turned the water black! She yanked her fingers through her hair to untangle it, then took up the comb, pulling hard enough to yank half the sopping hair off her head. But eventually it went through smoothly, and finally the water was dirtier than her skin.

She could barely look at Annabelle, at that firm, round belly. Of all the things that could happen in the world, this was the worst. She thought of all the men Annabelle'd let in and out. How Annabelle pulled away from those who refused to use the French letters she provided. How Annabelle got pregnant anyway. Annabelle was trapped now—not with a man—but with something growing in her. Too bad the herbs in Blackwell's didn't work. "What are you gonna do?"

"Don't have one damn idea. Get Tommy to marry me, I suppose. Go honest, least when it shows too much. I don't know."

"How the hell we gonna take care of it?"

"*We*?"

"We always said we wouldn't be stupid like that, Annabelle. You told me that. Now what? You're gonna marry Tommy? He ain't gonna marry you. He just wants his cut of the money you make."

"Stop."

"What about me? I kept the place for us. What about Brooklyn? What about our plan, that we was gonna start over?"

Annabelle rested against the back of the tub and closed her eyes. "I can't do this now."

"Get rid of it."

"No."

"Fine." Mollie stepped from the bath. She shrugged on her undergarment, and was about to put on the dress—but now that she was clean, she saw more clearly the muck that lay a good six inches up from the hem of her skirt. She held the dress over the tub, and began to rub it clean in the water.

"Washtubs for clothes are downstairs in the basement." The under matron glared at them from her seat. Her voluminous skirts and broad waist showed decades of fatty corned beef and very little cabbage. "Two cents extra."

"We don't have two cents. And we've got at least a minute left."

"First time here?"

Mollie shot a look at Annabelle. "Sure."

The under matron glanced at her colleagues to make sure they were occupied elsewhere. "Just this once, then."

The dirt did not come completely out of her skirt. Still, it was better than it had been. Mollie braided her hair and rolled it into a bun. She put on her coat.

Annabelle dried herself, then dressed. She looked flashy and bold, the material of her skirt too thin to be of much use but to pull up in an alley.

"Exit right at the bottom of the stairs," the under matron said. "God bless."

"And God damn," Mollie added.

At the new and rapidly expanding Cherry Street Settlement House, one was not allowed to exit the door through which one came. No, Mollie and Annabelle, who had come only for baths, were forced to trot by shining new classrooms, wherein sat women learning English ("How Do You Do?") and politics ("What Makes a Republican?") and proper raising of children ("Never Let the Child Rule"). The board near the exit was filled with many pieces of paper, offering lectures and classes on everything from the question of "the women's vote" to typewriting.

"Anything of interest?" There was a rustle of silk behind them. The woman who spoke was not much taller than Mollie. Her eyes were light blue and sharp behind her glasses.

The Do-Gooder. Miss DuPre. The rich bitch who had apparently just fired all the under matrons upstairs. One of those odd ones, with money and a college education, hell-bent on changing "the Poor."

"I'd be interested in knowing where we're gonna take baths," Mollie said, "now that you've removed them all."

"Just making room. As you can see from the board, we're adding classes. Sewing, reading, mathematics, typewriting, morals, housekeeping."

"I know cleanliness is next to godliness, but typewriting?"

"You teach reading?" Annabelle asked.

"And we have a board for jobs."

"We've got jobs, thank you," Mollie said. "I'm a thief and she's a whore. We could teach classes if you like."

The Do-Gooder frowned. "I thought you were an opium runner."

"A what?"

"Isn't that what you said last week?"

"I did?" Mollie shrugged. "Change in career."

"Are you a good thief?"

"Not too bad, if I do say so myself."

The woman looked as if she might laugh, but then her gaze flicked over Annabelle's stomach. She pulled a flyer from the board and offered it to Annabelle.

Mollie grabbed the paper. Annabelle grabbed the other end. "If you give it to me, I'll read it to you."

"If you come here," the woman said to Annabelle, "you can read it yourself."

On the way home, Annabelle stopped in the middle of the sidewalk. "I want to learn to read."

"Since when?"

"I want a better life. If I learn to read, maybe, just maybe—"

"So *I'll* teach ya. You want to be preached at all day by some do-gooder? Reading? Christ, Annabelle, what's happened to you?"

"I ain't going to jail again." She squeezed the bridge of her nose; her cheeks flushed pink.

"Aw, you gonna cry? You don't gotta go to jail again. Look, it's all right. We're gonna go meet the boys and have fun and everything's gonna be the way it was, all right?"

"But it's not the way it—"

"I *know* already. I know."

LEFTY MALONE'S DANCEHALL

IN THE BOWERY AND along Mulberry Street and Mott and Delancey and Chatham Square and Paradise Alley, in the empty lots and busy corners and dark walkways, there were many boys who claimed to be king. They swaggered in princely packs, in fours or fives or eights. They had grand names for themselves: Rum Runners, the Growlers, Black Hats, Guts and Glory. Each gang staked a territory and waited for their rivals to set foot in it. Should another group, whether by accident or design, happen by, bricks and bats and cans appeared from nowhere. And when the munitions were depleted, hard fists took their place. They fought until blood flowed and would have fought to the death, but usually a policeman or someone's father turned up.

Then a boy—usually the one with the bloodiest head—would get another beating from his father or a good smack of the policeman's wood baton. He would be sent home, cursing every step of the way.

The rival gangs would separate with only a can or two thrown as they went their different ways. General loafing would be the next activity, or perhaps a bit of gambling and a pail of beer passed among the swaggering princes.

The most revered boys were those whose pictures graced the *Police Gazette*. And of those, Tommy McCormack, lead fellow of the Growlers, took the prize. His photo had been seen three times in the newspapers; he cut the pictures out and kept them in his wallet for good luck. He had a beautiful face, did Tommy McCormack. Angelic, even, with his soft lips and clear blue eyes. Those eyes had gotten him released from court nearly every time.

Tommy McCormack, Hugh O'Dowd, and Seamus Feeney sat at a small round table right up front near the dancing women onstage. They wore hard, shiny black bowlers. Their stiff collars, pinned in the back by a single pearl stud, flapped loose like birds' wings. This was the mark of a Growler.

At Lefty Malone's, the stage wasn't much to speak of, but then again, the whole place wasn't much to speak of. Ribbons of red, white, and blue draped the walls; the fuzzy dust dated them from the Civil War, if not before. The walls themselves were black from cigarette smoke. The floors were warped and sticky, the chairs broken, the tables full of white rings. Tuesdays and Thursdays were ladies' nights, which meant old prostitutes came to dance with the patrons. Five cents a dance. The bill went higher for a feel (or more) in one of the small rooms down the hall.

Lefty served just enough food so as to remain within the liquor laws: two salted pigs' knuckles and two pieces of dark bread per table. Otherwise, he left the saloon alone. He preferred to let the Growlers keep the peace. He allowed Tommy to choose the dancing girls. He allowed Tommy to make the payoff to the police.

Annabelle Lee nuzzled Tommy's shoulder. Her fingers played with the blond hairs on the back of his neck. She wore the red dress. She had put on more makeup. Mollie thought she looked like a china doll next to Tommy, and she remembered how much this always bothered her. She was a different Annabelle Lee around the boys. She was the whore who smiled at the right times and kept her opinions to herself. But then Annabelle gazed at Tommy, and it wasn't a whore's lie, but something real and wanting and desperate. Waiting for a smile turned just her way. Looking for a small hint that her coming back meant something more than a warm body sometimes at night.

"You've got fat, Annabelle." Tommy took a sip of beer, set the mug down lightly. He removed a handkerchief from his jacket pocket and wiped his mouth. "Jail must've been good to you."

"I ain't fat." She shot a look to Mollie. "I look just the same's I went in, right?"

"Sure," Mollie said.

Annabelle ran the back of her hand along Tommy's cheek. "I ain't fat. And stop staring at the girls on the stage."

Tommy threw her a half smile and patted her leg.

"And I ain't a dog, so stop patting me."

Mollie rolled her eyes. Although she loved Annabelle, she had to admit that sometimes she was an idiot. And Annabelle was just at that point of being drunk where Mollie didn't know what she'd do.

Seamus ran his hand down Mollie's arm, and up again near her breast. She should have liked it, that simple and gentle touch. But all she wanted was some space and to sit up straight.

"Where ya going?" Seamus pulled her tighter.

"Here, Seamus, pick a card," Hugh said. "I'll guess what it is. If I'm right, you buy the beer." Hugh stuck his fingers in his vest pockets. He sported his hat at a steep angle, low upon his eye. He must have thought that made him look tough, but instead he looked like he was dressing in his father's clothes.

Seamus sniffed, winked at Mollie, and then pulled a card. He palmed it toward her. Three of spades.

"Now stick it back in the deck." Hugh stretched his arms, then shook out his fingers. He adjusted the daisy in the lapel of his yellow-and-black-checked suit. "Get ready to lose, my friend."

Hugh laid the cards face up in an arc. He ran his fingers over them, lightly tapping certain ones, then shaking his head. He stacked the cards, shuffled them, and pulled the top one from the deck. "Three of spades."

Seamus lit a cigarette, and then cuffed Hugh on the head.

"What the hell was that for?" Hugh's voice cracked; he was just that age. He picked his derby up off the sticky wood floor and jammed it on his head.

"Go get us another pail of beer," Seamus said.

"But I won."

"But I'm thirsty, see? It was the queen of hearts, dummy." Seamus rolled his lip in a sneer. "You need a little more practice. And your jacket's hurting my eyes." He glanced at Tommy for approval.

"I won," Hugh whined. "You lost. It was the three of spades. Mollie, it was the three of spades, right? Seamus is conning me."

Poor Hugh. It was a good trick; Mollie knew it herself and used to play it with the newsboys in the alley. "Try it again," she said to him.

"Forget it, I'm bored," Seamus said. "Go get the beer."

"You get it."

Seamus smiled, then flicked open a switchblade. He jabbed it into the table, piercing the card.

Hugh glared at Seamus. "You don't scare me. I'm saying you don't scare me. No matter how hard you try, you'll never scare me, Seamus Feeney."

"Go get the beer," Seamus said.

"No."

Seamus threw his cigarette in the floor, stood, and bent close into Hugh's face. "Oh, yeah?"

"Yeah."

Hugh flinched as Seamus grabbed him around the collar and twisted his shirt up tight. "Get the beer."

"You get it." Hugh's breath spluttered, and his face turned a purplish red.

With his free hand, Seamus pulled Hugh's ear. Hugh's arms flailed around and his feet could not find the ground.

"All right! All right."

Letting go, Seamus watched Hugh fall in a heap on the floor. Hugh coughed and spat. He wiped at his ear with the rag he kept as a handkerchief. He snaked out a hand and yanked Seamus's knife from the table.

Seamus held out his hand. The knife was still open; Hugh knew it and Seamus knew it. The thin blade shook in Hugh's grasp. He stared at Seamus's spread hand, taking in the nicotine yellow between his first and middle fingers, the calluses across the top of his palm, the soft skin below.

Seamus did not blink and did not move. He felt Hugh's eyes and he knew Hugh wanted to cut him.

The girls on the stage twirled in circles; the yellow of their silk petticoats set the men in the dancehall to cheering.

"Give him the knife, you bastard," Tommy said.

Hugh folded the blade into its sheath and gave the knife over. Seamus raised a hand at him, and then sat back down.

"Get us some beer," Tommy said.

"But— "

All Tommy McCormack had to do was rise slightly from his seat, and Hugh grabbed the empty pail and scuttled away.

Seamus shook his head and laughed. "Little bastard, thinks he can ..." His voice lost energy under Tommy's angelically cold stare. He swallowed hard.

"Was it the three of spades?" Tommy asked.

"Who cares what it was?"

"There's enough people to cheat without cheating your friends." Tommy glanced toward the bar, which curved like a horseshoe between the front doors. "Calhoun's here."

Seamus looked. "What's he doing here?"

"Fuck," Tommy said. "His boys are at each door."

Heavy feet thumped toward them. "Sorry I'm late. It was my sister's birthday. Ma had cake." Mugs Dennehy was huge, with a flattened nose and a box head that sported a hat a size too tight. "So what's with the Rum Runners paying a visit?"

Tommy slipped his knife back up his sleeve. "Goddamn Calhoun wants the saloon."

"Well, he's not gonna get it. He ain't getting anything on this block," Seamus said.

Tommy narrowed his eyes. He let go of Annabelle.

"Not tonight. I only been home a few hours. We were supposed to celebrate, Tommy."

"Have some more gin and shut up."

"Don't tell her to shut up," Mollie said.

"What're we going to do, Tommy?" Seamus asked. He had his hands in fists already.

"We'll go out the stage door."

"You saw the bricks in the alley?" Mugs asked. "We got a

lot." He wiped his coat sleeve against his nose and nodded to Annabelle. "Good to see ya back."

"I got the growler!" Hugh ran over and held the pail of beer, like an offering, to Tommy.

The boys all passed it around. Tommy raised his hand. "We got bricks. When the girls go off for their break, we walk out the stage door. The Rum Runners'll try and catch us outside. I don't want them thinking they can come in here anytime they please."

"Ya ruined this card, Seamus." Hugh waved the three of spades Seamus had speared, and then gathered the deck together.

Tommy took a pull of beer and smiled over at Calhoun. Calhoun glowered in return and turned his back.

Mollie stood. "Come on, Annabelle. Ain't no need for us here."

"It's early. I thought we were going to celebrate," Annabelle whined. "Can't you just leave it tonight, Tom?" Annabelle worked hard to keep her eyes focused. She squinted to see Calhoun. "Maybe he's just having a drink."

Tommy ignored her. "We go out when the girls go offstage. I'll walk out to the street alone. Draw Calhoun and his crew right to us."

The piano slammed out a final, jarring chord. Neely got up from the bench and pulled the rope to drop the curtain on the stage. Dust shook itself loose from the old moss-green curtains and mixed with the heavy smoke in the room.

Calhoun took a step forward. Tommy stood, his chair scraping the floor. There came the flick of knives opening at the Growlers' table.

Tommy nodded to the boys. It was time. He led them up the three small steps to the stage.

"Come on, Annabelle, we got to go." Mollie watched as Calhoun gave a short signal to his gang, who slid through the front doors.

"I want to celebrate." Annabelle picked up her glass, and when she realized it was empty, slammed it down on the table.

"You're drunk." Mollie put Annabelle's arm over her shoulder and lifted her. "Jesus, help me out a little. I ain't carrying ya out."

She half-dragged Annabelle up the stairs and onto the stage, then pushed the curtain aside to let them through.

"Tommy's got another girl, don't he?" Annabelle asked. "He's got to have, else why would he do this tonight?"

"Shhh."

"She's probably waiting for him right now. Why couldn't we have stayed inside? I liked the show." Annabelle's head rolled back, and then fell forward.

Mollie shook Annabelle's shoulders. "How much gin did you have?"

"Aw, leave it be, you ain't so sober yourself."

The dancing girls milled around them. As the girls dropped their pasted smiles like so much confetti and rubbed their worn feet, Tommy shoved open the alley door.

AGAINST THE RUM RUNNERS

THEY HUDDLED AGAINST THE alley wall. The windows of Lefty Malone's threw a yellow puddle across the street in front of them. Mollie heard the stamp of feet and the roars from inside; the girls were back onstage, likely showing more than their legs.

Mollie counted the neatly stacked bricks. "How many are there?" she asked.

"About fifty, I think," Mugs said. "We got about fifty, right, Seamus?"

"There's forty-two. Some kids ran off with some earlier. But I been checking them every day," Hugh said. He stroked the top layer as if it were a fighting dog about to go into the ring.

"Rum Runners. I meant how many Rum Runners."

"Six or seven. Not counting Calhoun." Hugh puffed as he tossed bricks to Seamus and Mugs. The boys each put one brick in their left coat pocket and one in their right. Then there came a brick per hand. "I'm gonna smack a brick right in his head, I tell ya. Coming inta Lefty's without an invite."

Mugs peered around the corner. He smacked his slungshot —a leather bag filled with lead pellets—against his palm. "I don't know," he said. "It's crowded out there."

"You saying I don't got good aim?" Hugh snapped. "You saying I'll miss one of those jacks and hit a kid or something?" His eyes were pink as a pig's belly—filled with alcohol and anxiety.

"Quiet," Seamus muttered.

"Shut up, Seamus." Hugh's lip curled.

"Wait for my signal." Tommy smoothed his hair and rubbed his shoes against the back of his pant legs. He struck a match against the bricks and lit a cigarette that flared red against his skin. He stepped into the pool of gaslight on the street, and leaned against the pole.

"There's more than seven of them," Mollie said.

"Shut up," Hugh hissed. "We're waiting for the signal." He shoved past Mugs and stuck his head out to the street. "Calhoun's out the door. I see him."

Mugs grabbed him by the collar and pulled him back. "Wait for the signal."

"Let's get'em." Hugh breathed heavily. "I'm sick of em."

"I'm sick of em, too," Mugs said.

"I'm gonna flatten that Calhoun, I swear I will—"

"Those sons of—"

"Don't deserve this street, do they—"

"I've wanted to get Calhoun for so long—"

"Get'em—"

"Hurt'em—"

"I'll kill them all—"

"Now?" Hugh called to Tommy. "Now, Tommy?"

Tommy McCormack shook his head. Then he pushed off the lamppost, taking one step forward. He tossed aside his cigarette.

Calhoun came into view. He was shorter than Tommy, a lump next to Tommy's sleek figure. He stopped directly in front of him and stared.

"Now?" Hugh asked.

"Wait for the signal," Seamus whispered.

Hugh watched Tommy. "He's letting Calhoun walk by ..."

"He won't get away—" Mugs said.

"He *will*. Tommy's gonna let him walk right on by and the whole thing'll be ruined. He's gonna let him walk—"

"Shut up," Mugs said.

Then Hugh did it. He grabbed a brick and slung it into the street. "*Now!*"

Mugs and Seamus joined in, grabbing bricks and throwing them with all their might.

On the street, Calhoun covered his head and dashed behind a cart. Someone's brick caught the horse pulling the cart, and the animal broke out in a gallop, the cart tilting and swaying behind it, spilling vegetables everywhere. People on the street scattered, finding doorways and alleys to escape the rain of the bricks.

"We're running you off, Calhoun!" Hugh called out. "All of youse can just—" He hefted another brick, which went off course, crashing through a milliner's window.

Seamus grabbed Hugh around the neck and wrestled him to the ground. "You stupid—you wait for the signal! Jesus, you idiot"

"Let go, I can't breathe!"

"Go!" Mugs loped forward.

"Go go go!" Tommy yelled, not only to urge the boys on, but to warn anyone in their way to move aside.

Then the fists flew, because the Rum Runners were out in full force—Mollie counted eight of them. Hugh went down first and started blubbering. Someone kicked Mugs in the back and then got a boot to his face. Seamus flung short punches and was quick enough to dodge fists. But there were too many of them; they kept yelling and punching, sending Mugs to the ground once more.

The bricks were forgotten, Hugh having messed everything up. A crowd circled the boys; they taunted and jeered. Broken bottles had become the new weapon. Mugs whirled around with his slungshot bag of lead pellets. A boy no older than ten flew at Seamus, his eyes full of fury and hate.

Seamus froze.

Stupid to freeze, with the Rum Runners getting the upper hand. Stupid enough to get a brick smacked in the back of the head. He crumpled. His cheek scraped the pavement. He tried to get up, but his arms and legs went all different directions.

"Seamus!" Mollie called.

A police whistle squealed.

"Seamus!" Mollie rushed forward, but Annabelle grabbed her coat and pulled her back.

"Don't leave me here."

"But Seamus—Jesus, let go of me."

"Mugs's got him, see?"

It was true. Mugs lifted Seamus from the ground, tried to drag him away. Hugh joined him.

The gangs scattered in all directions. Three policemen ran up. The onlookers pointed every which way, but the policemen just started swinging their nightsticks into the crowd and arrested anyone who fell.

Annabelle pulled Mollie farther into the alley, between

the steps to the stage door and an ash barrel. Mollie heard yells and thwacks from the street.

"It's all ruined, ain't it?" Annabelle turned in a circle, stumbled, then caught herself up with a hand on the brick wall. Above her head was a faded and torn poster for Annie Hindle, dressed to the nines and tipping her hat like the gentleman she certainly wasn't. Below her image, Annabelle swayed. Her eyes were rimmed with red, and her blond wig hung askew. "Who's he seeing, Mollie? Whose hole is he plugging now? Goddamn shit of a man."

"No one. He ain't seeing no one." A spit of wind shook the poster; Annie Hindle seemed to wink. As if she had witnessed Tommy McCormack's exit with one, two, three dancers.

"I saw him looking at the redhead on the stage. Tits to Timbuktu."

"He wasn't looking at no girl."

Annabelle tilted her head and smiled. "Let's go down to the docks, Moll. Roll us some sailors who'll be happy"—and this she spat—"for the company. So Tommy thinks we'll show up at the boardinghouse and bandage all their wounds. Pat'em, kiss'em, and fuck'em so they feel like kings."

"Annabelle ..."

"Well, there's plenty more where they came from and plenty more that will pay. Shouldn't give it away anyway, right? Only gets you stuck. I don't feel good." She pressed her back against the wall and pulled in a knot of air. "I don't know what's worse. The hell I just left or this. God, I'm drunk, Moll."

Yes, drunk the way Mollie hated most. The drunk where she had to keep Annabelle from opening her legs to a room full of strangers who offered nothing more than quick wisps of love and few cents and maybe a stale beer. The type of drunk that hated everyone and anything and especially herself. She stepped forward and grabbed Annabelle's arms. "We're going home."

"Are you my mother? 'Cause I got one already."

"Who you ain't seen since you were nine years old."

"What do you—"

A dark figure charged down the alley, lit only from the streetlight behind him. His breath was sharp and hard.

"Tommy?" Annabelle asked.

Too broad to be Tommy. Too short to be Mugs. Too thin to be Hugh.

"'*Tommy*?'" There was a sneer in the man's voice as he mimicked Annabelle. "Not Tommy."

Calhoun.

Annabelle leaned back against the ash barrel, her fingers grasping the metal rim. "Give ya a feel for ten cents."

"Ya will, huh?" Calhoun sauntered closer, his breath filled with liquor. He looked Annabelle up and down and stepped in close.

"Get out of here, Calhoun," Mollie said.

But he didn't listen, just grabbed Annabelle's skirt and pushed it up around her waist.

"Ya want me, don't ya?" Annabelle whispered. "But I'm a good girl now. Like Mollie. So just a feel."

His hand went between her legs. Annabelle jerked and gritted her teeth.

Mollie punched him in the back. "She said a feel."

"I'm giving her a feel."

"It's enough." She grasped at Annabelle's arm, but Calhoun caught her wrist. "Leave her alone."

Annabelle tuned toward Mollie, her eyes black with alley light, empty. "Go home, Mollie."

Calhoun pushed Mollie away. She stepped backwards. "Please, Annabelle ..."

"Go home."

"I'll be waiting on the street."

Calhoun sauntered out. He looked around at the lights, then spat. He reached into the pocket of his loose jacket and tossed a three-cent coin toward Mollie. "Got herself a guardian angel. Lucky girl."

AFTERNOON

THE NEXT AFTERNOON, MOLLIE set the bucket under the second-floor spigot and turned the handle all the way. Not that it made much difference in the amount of water coming out.

Annabelle had been sick the night before—didn't she know not to mix gin and beer?—and then sick all morning. Damn Friday morning—best day on Hester Street for a bit of pickpocketing—and here Mollie stood getting water to clean up the mess. She heard the minutes ticking away, as if a watch swung by her ear. All the good minutes, when the groceries were fresh and pockets and purses full. *Annabelle had best be standing by the time I get back upstairs, she thought. She'd better be ready to go.*

Next to her, a mother scrubbed her son, who sat cross-legged in the sink. She wiped at him with a rag, and then squeezed the cloth over his head. Mollie'd never seen them before.

"Just move here?" she asked the mother.

"From the front building. Water pipe's busted."

The little boy was pink and smiling, splashing his mother, who flicked the cloth at him and mopped her face with her apron.

He slapped his hand in the basin water. Some of it landed on Mollie's skirt. "Watcha doing?"

"Getting water."

"Why?"

"Why not?"

The little boy held on to the rolled sides of the metal sink and pulled himself up. His skin was covered in goose pimples.

"You look like a plucked chicken," Mollie said.

He leaned toward her. "Yer ugly."

"Ian!" His mother swatted him with the rag. "Sorry."

"She's ugly," Ian said.

"Well, you're so ugly your real mam left you and this one's a banshee. Might just drown you if you don't look out," Mollie said.

"Not a banshee."

"How do ya know?" Mollie asked. "You ever asked her?'

The boy stuck out his bottom lip. He looked up at his mother, the first signs of mistrust shadowing his eyes.

"Well, go ahead, ask her."

His mother set her hands on her hips. "That's enough," she said to Mollie.

"Ask her," Mollie hissed.

"You a banshee?" His eyes were round with fright.

"No, now, we're done." She glared at Mollie, then lifted little simple Ian from the sink and wrapped her apron around him. He grasped her around the middle with his legs. Oh, but he didn't take his eyes from his mother's face. And then his lower lip trembled and twisted. Tears and a scream burst forth.

"You ought to be ashamed of yourself."

Mollie winked at the boy. "Yer a brave one, I'll tell you that. Love yer ma well and she won't bite." Mollie popped a matchstick in her mouth, grabbed her own bucket, and took the stairs two at a time.

But there Annabelle lay, curled tight on the bed. Her skin was ashen, her eyes ringed in black. Her red dress lay on the floor in a heap.

"Ain't ya up yet? We got work to do."

"Go yourself."

Mollie poured some water into a pot to boil. "I'm making you potatoes. And I'm gonna only be nice this once, 'cause you just got out of jail."

"I hate potatoes."

"It's all we've got, so don't complain."

Annabelle ran the tip of her tongue over her lips. "I'm thirsty."

"I'll get you tea when the water boils. A beer'd make you feel better, but there ain't one, so you'll have to make so."

"This isn't from the drink. I been sick like this for weeks. Matron at the infirmary said it was common. It don't last long."

"We'll have to give the dress a soak." Mollie poured water into the teacup. "Here, plain water'll be better for you."

Annabelle pushed herself up and reached fort the cup. She leaned back against the wall and sighed, watching Mollie put the potatoes in the pot. "I'm going to that settlement house today."

"Why?"

"I want to read."

"Reading ain't gonna get us to Brooklyn. When we get there, you can take all the time you want to read."

Annabelle stuck out her chin. "I want to learn *now*. You don't listen to me."

"I'll teach ya. You don't need some charity place for that."

"How?"

"Look at the walls, Annabelle. I changed the papers on them right before you came home. There's a great story going on—*The Nick McFadden Adventure.*"

"Read it to me."

Mollie crossed to the papers and found the pink pages of the *Police Gazette*. "It's good, see? Listen—"

PART THREE:

WHEREIN NICK MCFADDEN IS
SHANGHAIED
AGAINST HIS WILL!

> The bag dropped on little Nick's head before he could even say a prayer. Trapped! Against his will and God knew where the kidnappers would take him. His friend Marlowe had warned him of such things, and he thought he had been careful. But now he felt his hands and legs tied, felt himself thrust into the back of a cart, to be taken away from all he knew and loved. Tears coursed his cheeks, and he wiped them against the muslin that blocked the real world from his sight.

"The nuns at them charity houses you were always getting kicked out of taught you to read," Annabelle said.

"So?"

"So how come I can't go to some charity house and learn, too?"

Mollie stirred the water, spinning the potatoes in a circle. "The sooner we get out on the street, the sooner we'll make enough money for Brooklyn. We need the money, Annabelle. We need that more. Besides, I'm feeling lucky. I want to bet on that new dog at the Rat Pit."

Annabelle rubbed her eyes. "Jesus, I don't even know if it's day or eve in here. It's as bad as the cell."

"It's what we got, Annabelle. It wasn't so easy keeping it. I got some debts."

"What do you mean?'

"Tommy's been fronting me money the last coupla months."

"Fronting you or giving you?"

"We don't take charity, do we? Not even from friends."

"How much?"

"Twenty dollars."

"Twenty dollars?"

"I thought I'd pay him back, easy. Just had a bad run of pockets. You know how it is."

"Well, you're not gonna pay it back. Once I tell Tommy about this baby, you know he'll forgive the loan."

"I think he'll just raise his cut of your wages."

"I know Tommy."

"Yeah, I guess you do." The room grew damp with steam as the potatoes boiled, and it brought out the stench of the bucket where Annabelle had been sick.

All Mollie needed was one deep pocket and very light hands. And the luck of the Irish—which had never been very good. But just a small amount of luck—that was all she needed—and she'd pay Tommy back and she and Annabelle would walk right straight across that new Brooklyn Bridge. Look at trees instead of gray laundry. Find a house with a window. Sleep in a soft shaft of sunlight.

But that took work, and it was time to begin.

Annabelle stood. She took her blue dress from the wall and pulled it over her head. Mollie pulled the stays tight.

Annabelle was silent. She took a long time applying her lip paint, twice veering off course and staining her chin. She rubbed her red shoes to a luster. "I want to quit this."

"Later. I promise. When we got enough money to move to Brooklyn."

NIGHTLIFE

"THERE—SEE IT?" MOLLIE and Annabelle stood in the alcove of a building, in front of a door to a women's hat shop. Mollie put her face to the glass, and let her eyes adjust. The gaslight from the street cast a sheen of silver throughout the room. Long mirrors reflected a settee and chairs curved to accommodate bustles, near a large oval carpet of white swans and blushing roses. Along the counter, the latest fashions adorned gilt hat stands. There was the oval midnight-blue bonnet with trails of lace. A mourning hat next—quite somber, quite simple, only the rich velvet giving away its price. Mollie peered farther. Where was it? Had it been bought? She looked for the hat with colors that could not easily be named, for its fabric changed from red to silver to gold depending on the mood of the sun. Where was the translucent lace that seemed like angel's wings? With the small stuffed bird taking flight from the crown?

There—nearly lost in the dark at the far end of the counter. "Right there—at the end. See it?"

"Goddamn, that's a slammer of a hat."

"Ain't it?" Mollie sighed. It was a beautiful hat. Completely useless. Yet it calmed her to see it still there each time she came to this doorway. The first time, she had wanted to steal it. She sneaked into the alley, looking for any vulnerable entrance. The door to the yard was metal, with a great metal lock. Thick bars guarded the long windows, and thin as she was, she knew she could not squeeze between them. She returned to the front, stared at the lock there, kneeling to view the tumblers, but the light was never quite bright enough, and what she saw looked complicated.

For weeks before Annabelle came home, in the hush hours between night and morning, when the only sounds were the scrabble of rats and the creaks of the mortar and brick, Mollie lay alone in bed and imagined herself wearing the hat. She was always strolling, never afraid, and the sky was always clear. The shade that dappled the sidewalk came from trees, not tenements. She took deep breaths of air, and it tasted like lemon candy. Men tipped their derbies as she passed; women shot envious glances. She was beautiful in the hat with the bird on its crown.

But then the city awoke around her. The Italians clanged open their stove, the hallway doors screeched and slammed as people descended to their jobs in tanneries and silver-plating factories and millineries and groceries. She rose, lit a candle, prodded the coal in the stove if there was coal, ate an apple if there was an apple. She marked another line on the wall, counted the marks, and figured the days until Annabelle's return. Combed and pinned her hair. Looked at herself in the bit of mirror.

Mollie knew she would never steal the hat. A hat like that needed a cloak, not a simple coat. And then there was the need for a dress of equal caliber, and a corset, and gloves, and stockings of fine wool. And a room with a window, so she might admire the shifting colors of the hat as it played with the light. So many impossible things.

She sighed and turned from the doorway. "Meet ya home later."

It was night now. It was the Bowery. It was time for Annabelle to flip her curls and catch the gaze of a stranger. It was time to play.

Two weeks. Two weeks since Annabelle came home. Two weeks of lousy pockets for Mollie, and for Annabelle, very few johns.

They had only sixty-eight cents left. Earlier in the day, twenty cents had gone for grilled sausages, pickled cabbage, and black bread at a café on the Bowery. For the last week, Annabelle had eaten two full meals a day. Annabelle seemed to always need two meals now.

The streetlight hissed, and its glow turned the sidewalk a pale gray. Mollie raised her eyes to the sound of horses and carriages drawing across the cobblestones and stopping before a theater that blazed with light. Men in tall black hats and heavy coats stepped from the carriages, handing out ladies with dainty hands and fur-lined jackets. The couples picked their way carefully through the fast freezing slush as the temperature dropped.

The crowd swelled, all the patrons waiting their turn to pass through the beaded glass doors. Mollie waited until the crowd was a swarm of satin and silk and wool, waited until everyone's focus was on only the broad doors that would lead to heat and a night's entertainment. She rubbed her hands, blew on them, flexing them, then stepped from the dark of her hiding place and moved between the carriages. The horses in their leathers hung their heads or munched from grain bags. The drivers lit cigarettes and wrapped their scarves tighter around their necks. They milled among one another, stamping their feet. Their breath hung in the air.

She moved in, her soft soles giving nothing away. The gentlemen would have their wallets in their chest pockets; the ladies would hide their rings in the muffs that warmed their hands. The easiest thing to take would be cuff links, or easing a watch from its pocket and slipping the chain from a vest button. The ladies might have a pocket in their skirts—might be a few coins there, too. She sidled into the crowd. She did not look at faces, but waists and wrists and pockets. She heard nothing but the rush of blood in her chest.

A little shove. A cuff link unclasped and in the pocket. Step away, run into a woman, apologize, slide a hand in her husband's jacket; yes, there's the leather. Slide the bills out under your coat, drop the wallet to the ground, let it be trampled by the crowd pushing impatiently forward now. A gold-and-black waistcoat, covering an ever-so-large stomach. Look at the watch chain beckon! Slide out the knife, only one slice to pop the button holding it. Down comes the watch into an open hand.

Her heart beat faster. She was close to the doors now—one more, one more something—but what? There—just the faint hint of an opening to a lady's pocket. Mollie let her go by, darting a hand in, coming up with a handkerchief and a miniature book. A Bible. She'd give them both to Annabelle as a present, for they were worthless to fence.

Her breath was shallow. Her ears filled suddenly with the murmurs of the latecomers rushing up. The cologne and perfume changed the air to streaks of gold.

She strode quickly away, back into the midst of the carriages. The drivers no longer lounged around, but had stepped inside their cabs for the wait. Only the horses bore witness to her passing.

Turning right at the hat shop, Mollie thought of the girls who would be clocking in before the sun. Who would wear their fingers to the bone and be old before they'd turned twenty. *Poor fools*, she thought. At least she had the freedom to see the sun, to wake when she wanted. She pulled out the cuff link she'd just stolen, flipped it in the air, caught it between two fingers, and kissed it.

The flagstones of the alley sloped inward to an open gutter, littered with ice, mud, and trash. The view of the sky above was knife-thin, for the buildings were solid brick, four stories each side.

Mollie lifted her skirts and was careful where she stepped. A black rat crawled from the gutter, stared at her with its shiny eyes, then scurried across her path and under a muslin sack of garbage.

She passed the first door with the shattered lantern, and came to a half door of weathered wood that showed in flecks and streaks that it had once been painted jade green. It had neither light above it nor knob upon it, and the brick wall that stopped the alley short kept the entrance in perpetual darkness. She knocked twice, then once. Waited three seconds. Gave four short raps. This was the abode of Black Jim, whose face was known by no one.

A small square was cut in the wood. It was pushed open by a hand with long fingers and threadbare cuffs. The odor of sour eggs and stale tobacco smoke followed. The hand turned, palm up; the nails were edged with crescents of black. She placed the cuff link in it. The fingers closed like a vise; the little opening was shut tight.

Mollie waited. She looked up at the sliver of night sky and the stars that pulsed and flickered. She stuck out a shoe and was annoyed at the splatters of mud on the leather.

The little door opened. Five cents.

"Not enough," she said.

Black Jim's hand held the coin between his index finger and thumb and did not move.

After pocketing the coin, she pulled the watch from her coat and gave it over. Waited again.

Two dollars. The bills fluttered.

"That's silver. The chain alone's worth—"

The hand and money disappeared.

The clear air brought cold. Mollie hopped from one foot to the other to bring up heat. She was certain this watch would bring at least twenty dollars, perhaps thirty, for it was beautiful and the tick was close to silent, the innards well designed. There would be money for Tommy, for food, for rent, for a bet at the Rat Pit.

Five dollars were proffered.

She grabbed the bills and stuffed them into the large pocket of her coat. "Tight-ass."

The door slammed shut.

His groan echoed in her chest. His heartbeat thumped against her. The cast-iron bed frame squealed, then slowed, then stopped. Seamus's leg remained heavily over hers, and the rough of his trousers scraped against her thigh.

She sat up and pushed down her skirts, organizing the folds until the fabric was smooth.

"Don't get up," he said. "Jesus, it's heaven just like this."

She gazed down at him. Such soft kisses he gave. And nights at the Rat Pit, or walks along the waterfront to see the ever-growing bridge. Simple kindnesses. He never forced her to do anything—not at all like other men. For hadn't she enough of that, of walking down the wrong alley, smiling at the wrong man, staying too long at a charity house Mass, compromising with a cop?

But with Seamus, for brief moments alone and touching, she could let the weight of the city fall from her.

Running a finger along his soft cheek, she thought, *I could love him.*

"Mmmm." He turned on his side. "Yer a beaut, Mollie Flynn."

"Ain't so bad-looking yourself, Seamus Feeney. Now that your head's healed up. Can't believe you let a Rum Runner nail you. Had to have hurt like hell."

Seamus reached to the night stand, picked up a cigarette, and lit it.

"Didn't hurt as much as that shit hurt when I found him."

"They'll try again."

"Maybe." Seamus smirked. "We paid a visit to Calhoun's little brother—Edgie Moore?"

"Yeah?"

"Just paid him a visit at his place of employment, that's all. He won't be working at the slaughterhouse for a while. Gotta take care of finding a new nose."

Mollie closed her eyes. "Jesus."

"No sirree. Handkerchief ain't gonna help him." Seamus sat up and shook his head. "I hate Calhoun. I hate everyone he's ever known. And they ain't gonna squeeze us out of Lefty's. I'll slit the throat of every one of the bastards before I'll let that happen."

Mollie heard the words, and knew they were not his, but Tommy's. He never questioned anything Tommy said or did. It was pathetic. Mollie wondered if he ever had a thought of his own. She remembered once that she'd asked him if he liked plum pudding. He'd looked around the room, instinctively settling on Tommy. Waiting for an answer. He didn't get one. He just shrugged his shoulders and turned the conversation to something else.

"I gotta go" Mollie said.

"Why?"

"'Cause I got to." How could she say that she loved one side of Seamus and hated the other? The other would win. It always did.

"Stay the night."

"You know me and Annabelle got a pact. You know—"

"I know," Seamus muttered. "Gotta come home at night."

"So's we know the other's all right."

Seamus sighed. He stretched out an arm and wrapped it around Mollie's waist.

"I gotta go." She brushed his arm aside and turned so her feet dropped over the side of the bed. She pulled on her shoes, and in her hurry knotted up one of the laces. She stood, took her coat from the hook in the door, and slung it on.

"See you later." She did not kiss him before leaving.

The Ragpickers' Lot was a narrow strip of empty space that ran from Roosevelt straight back to Chambers. It had not changed in the years since Annabelle had found her there. Only the faces were different. A few metal barrels of burning firewood provided the only warmth.

The right side of the lot was a marvel of technical design: Layers of scrap wood had been nailed or balanced to create sleeping quarters four squat levels high. It was a feat of design because it rarely collapsed. When it did, the thing seemed to build itself up within a day, and all the stalls were occupied. Long and narrow feet clad in mismatched socks stuck out of one box, fourth level. One ground-floor unit boasted a guard dog, who kept one eye open and one cropped ear cocked.

The left side of the lot held the rags—three men high and six deep—rags collected from trash bins for too many years to count. Some were washed in the nearby tub and resold.

Mollie wondered if they held children still, as they had once held her. She knew that men and women came often from the Children's Aid Society, that they brought broom handles to sift through the rags and find the children. Some of the Ragpickers would watch, and if a child was found, they would claim to be the boy's or girl's guardian and ask for fees before releasing the child. Most of the kids came back within a week. Others were not heard from again. The Children's Aid Society claimed to send the children to families in the West. But there was no one to prove that, and a lot of the kids thought they were being sold into white slavery.

Which in a way would be true, for the Society would clean them up, teach them to read and curtsy and sew and hammer, and find them a job. The do-gooders loved to boast about finding jobs for the "destitute." They boasted of the "honor of work," and how they'd steered another poor soul from the "depravities of crime." But work—in a factory, as a cash girl at a department store, as a maid in a Washington Square manse—meant only slavery in another form. Mollie herself had once asked after a job sewing ladies' gloves—only to find the wages so low one could barely afford a berth in a flophouse.

She crossed the lot, stopping at the first ash bin. An old man warmed his fingers, keeping them so low to the flame, Mollie thought his skin would singe black. One side of his body lifted higher than the other, like a puppet on strings. The left side of his mouth was pulled in a grimace, revealing more blank space than teeth.

"Hail Mary," he said to Mollie in that funny voice of his, half water and half wheeze. "Hail Mary full of grace." He set a fire-hot hand on her forehead. "Good to see you, Mary Mary Quite Contrary."

"Hey, Jip."

He removed his hand; the night seemed even colder than before. The rag mound sighed, as if the children sleeping there had let go of all their dreams at once. Mollie felt its heaviness and fear wrap around her. She knew what it was like; she understood the terror that kept them curled like dogs as far back into the rags as possible.

"Hail Mary got a penny for a pint?"

She reached into her breast pocket and handed Jip a handful of coins. Then she pulled out a dollar bill, rolling it tight. She set it in Jip's palm. His skin felt like paper, like autumn leaves. "Get some food for the kids in there, all right?"

He shoved the money in a grubby pocket. Nodded once. "Hail Mary full of grace, how does your garden grow? With silver shells and cocks and belles and Jesus' little toes." He held his hands over the fire again. His red-lined eyes slid toward the street and then snapped back to stare in the popping flames. "Got an admirer, Mary."

Mollie turned around. Tommy McCormack leaned against the broken fence, smoking. The glow of the cigarette's tip lit the blue in his eyes. She wanted, more than anything, to keep walking, to pretend she hadn't seen him. Just keep walking until she came to Chambers Street. From there, she had her choice of alleys or cellars to sneak through. But the worst thing you could do with Tommy was to show fear. She squared her shoulders, took a deep breath, and walked over to him. As if she knew he'd been following her all along.

"Got a penny for a pint?" He expelled smoke from his lungs, like he was on fire from within. Then he dropped the cigarette, and slowly ground it out with the bottom of his shiny shoes. "Or how about twenty dollars, which I believe you promised me last week."

"If I had it, I'd give it to you, wouldn't I?"

"I assume you'd give it to me, before you gave it to people like *that*." He smiled down at her, looking to all the world like a kind brother, concerned about her health.

"I don't got it right now. Give me another week. It'll be easy now that Annabelle's back, you know, now that she's working again. We're just a little tight right now."

"Annabelle." Tommy smiled. "Annabelle's let me down a bit lately. A lot lately."

"It's slow."

"She's lazy."

Tommy stepped forward, then circled around Mollie until he had her pressed against the fence. He leaned into her, his cheek touching hers, and his breath blew against her ear. "Got a job for ya, Moll. You do it, we'll call the debt even, all right?"

"What is it?"

"Chandler shop on Spring. You're the only one small enough to fit through the one window that's never shut. All you got to do is lift some keys from the watchman's pocket and open the front door."

"And what if the watchman catches me?"

"You got a knife, don't you?"

"It ain't for that."

"He won't see you. I been watching him. Drinks until he sleeps. And your fingers are the lightest around."

"I don't know."

Tommy shoved his hand under her coat, into the pocket. "What's this?"

Mollie winced. The money from black Jim and a couple other takes.

His fingers caught up the bills. He licked his index finger and counted. "Seven dollars. I'll take it as interest."

"That's rent money."

He tilted his head. "You're getting slow, aren't you? I took you for a talent at one time. Now I'm not so sure."

"I know you don't care one way or the other about me. But don't take away the rent money. I'll pay you back, I swear to god."

He hesitated, then folded the money in half and placed it back in her coat. "Guess it's twenty-seven you owe me now. I want it next week. Unless you decide to play with me. It's just a matter of opening a door. Thought you'd like the challenge." He lifted his derby to her and started for the street. "Oh, and tell Annabelle I miss her. I can trust you to tell her that, can't I?"

He swaggered away, whistling some tune as he went.

HOW MOLLY FLYNN CAME TO BE

SHE HAD BEEN TOLD many stories, some simple, some filled with wonder. Her favorite story began with a beautiful woman and a million stars.

The beautiful woman was her mother; her name was Calliope. She had light hair that shined in the moonlight. Her eyes were light, too, and if anyone took the time, they'd see all her thoughts and secrets. Calliope tried to keep many secrets. But her eyes gave her away, and Mollie often damned her, for her own eyes were just the same.

Calliope's big secret was Mollie. Calliope was a lady, still under her father's fine roof. She was promised to an older man with graying whiskers and ten thousand dollars in the bank. They had never so much as held hands.

Calliope would sit in the parlor on a horsehair-and-velvet couch, listening to the tick of a rosewood clock, reading some bit of poetry. Her left hand held the book to the light. Her right hand was spread across herself, her palm feeling the tiny beat of Mollie's heart.

As Mollie grew bigger and bolder inside her (for Mollie was quite a courageous child—that's what the Sister had told her), Calliope paid her maid ten dollars to sew her dresses with lace and roses and many flounces meant to hide her secret.

On Saturdays she was handed into a shiny brougham that took her around Central Park. She threw bread to the birds.

When it was time for Mollie to appear in the world, Calliope walked from Washington Square to the Lower East Side. The heels on her soft leather boots tore off somewhere, and soon Calliope stumbled. There were men looking her over, staring with loneliness from under the brims of their slouch caps. Others were half drunk with whiskey, half drunk with greed, who saw her silk dress and wondered if here was money clinking in a pocket or two. But then she'd walk under an oil lamp, and those men would see the blood staining the fine fabric and they'd turn away.

She could barely breathe. The sweat that matted her hair did not come from the heavy July heat, but from Mollie, now writhing and twisting, trying to tear her mother in two.

She finally reached the river. The tight streets and tilting wood buildings ended. In front of her, ships swayed in their moorings. She breathed to the creak of wood hulls and prayed to the tall masts, which looked much like the crosses in the church, what with their sails furled and only their vulnerable skeletons showing.

And then Mollie came—too soon, before Calliope was ready. She had meant to drown them both in the river. Instead, her child slid from her body to the street and down the slope to the water, in an oily mess of blood that would not stop flowing.

Calliope grabbed the cord, that lifeline between mother and child, and tor at it with her teeth. She watched Mollie slide away.

Mollie fell into the water with a tiny splash. There were a million stars that night, wondrous stars, God's light welcoming her to the world. Mollie knows her mother would have saved her, had she not died in the act of letting go. She does not remember the nun who found her and scooped her from the rushes. Fat, fat baby floating like a fallen star near the river's edge.

This was the story Sister Mary Clara told her. Mary Clara was dismissed from the charity for telling such gruesome lies to little girls. At Mary Clara's charity, Mollie went by the name of Sarah.

The story Mollie Flynn liked the least was probably the truth. She had been left in the basket outside the foundling Asylum, lucky enough not to freeze during the night. She was given the name of Margaret.

She had been called Alice and Caroline and even Pennsylvania. Charity to charity, outgrowing one, transferred to another after stealing bread, kicked out from a third for "seducing" the priest at Mass. She'd learned the skills of pickpocketing from Googs Mallory, whose bed was next to hers in the New York School for Delinquent Children. Googs was the only one who believed Mollie's story. She was also familiar with Father Timothy's roving hands.

They escaped together, and Mollie became the "stall," shifting a mark's attention away from his wallet long enough for Googs to take it. Then one morning, Googs disappeared with money that by all rights should have been shared.

* * *

Not much she could do after that but learn the trade better. At first, she supplemented her earnings of pennies by begging, then singing on a street corner and gasping as if she were to die of consumption any minute. She knew all the saloons with the deepest and freshest trash bins. She kept to herself—how Father Timothy had set her against trusting anyone!—and crawled into the mound of rags in the Ragpickers' Lot for sleep. She woke and wandered and became the best pickpocket she could.

Each morning, she emerged to find a cup of beer and some scrap of food—a half-eaten muffin, a rip of ham, an apple. As she ate, she watched a girl across the lot who wore a blonde wig and lifted her skirts in daylight. She knew this girl was the one who brought food.

Mollie once asked Annabelle why she chose to rescue her. "Hell," Annabelle said, "I used to sleep in that very same spot when my da and mam threw me over for the new baby. I just didn't want no one else to take it, that's all. Never know when I'll need it again. Just want the space free, is all."

And she saw in Annabelle Lee the kindest person she'd ever known.

March 1883

A FORTUNE

"IT'S JUST A MATTER OF opening a door, Annabelle. He's gonna take it as payment for the debt. Jesus, that sets us up right. Then what we take is our own again. If we're lucky, we'll have enough to move by summer.

Annabelle stared through the window of a secondhand shop at a tortoiseshell comb and a pair of gloves that showed only the slightest wear on the fingers. "I got a bad feeling, is all."

"I go through a window. I lift a set of keys. I unlock a door. I walk out."

"Don't you ever wonder what it'd be like to be honest?"

"I'm honest. And we're honestly broke. And it's Sunday and I don't want to think about it." Mollie continued down the street. She massaged her temples. She wanted to squeeze out the thoughts, the ones that came unbidden, the ones that kept her from Mass, that kept her from sleep.

She was a thief because it paid better than a real job. It

was a job, and she was of a practical nature. She knew what it took to survive—how much to steal to make rent, to buy food, to have a few odd coins for enjoyment. She had analyzed the streets of the Fourth Ward, the movement of the people, and determined the best times of day to maximize her take. She had been cautious and never greedy. And she loved the challenge—yes, she admitted it—loved the way her fingers tingled and sounds flattened out and the only things she saw were pockets and purses. But the faces of the people came to her at night, and she felt guilt then, like hot ashes.

Annabelle came up beside her. She kept her hands crossed over her stomach. The baby was obvious now.

"You're gonna have to tell Tommy, instead of avoiding him and the dancehall," Mollie said.

"He's avoiding me, too."

"Yeah, well."

"I'm not gonna be able to work much longer."

"I know." Mollie felt a thick pain begin in her head.

"I'm gonna need to do something else."

"Then be my stall. You know how to do that."

"I mean after that, Moll. When we're in Brooklyn. I want a job. I'm sick of men touching me. And I can't do it—not with a baby."

"A job. That's funny."

"What does that mean?"

"You been walking the streets all your life. You tell me what else you can do."

Annabelle stopped in her tracks. "Fuck you, Mollie Flynn."

Mollie knew she shouldn't have said it, but she also knew it was true. Or had been, until the goddamn baby. Until the money on the table had started to dwindle to dimes and quarters. "I'm sorry."

Annabelle walked away from Mollie, then turned on the heel of her red shoe and said, "I can change. And one day I'm gonna be able to walk straight into Mass and not have one goddamn sin to confess."

"I said I was sorry."

"Do the job for Tommy. I don't care."

Mollie watched the bounce of curls as Annabelle stomped away.

"Buy a flower or your future?"

Mollie started. She turned to the rumpled figure in the doorway.

A woman sat cross-legged, a spread of cards in the rags of her skirt. The crown of her head was mottled brown and pink, showing through tufts of white hair. She raised her gaze to Mollie; her eyes were milky and blind. The red paint on her lips crept into the crevices age had dug around her mouth. A basket of spring's first wildflowers, obviously pulled from an empty lot, edged with the brown of frost and sighing over the sides, rested nearby.

"Well, hell. Hermione Montreal," Mollie said. How often she and Annabelle had sat in Hermione's burgundy -festooned apartment, sneezing at the dust, and giggling from the whiskeys she'd proffered them.

"Ah, my fame precedes me. Flower or future?"

"What happened to you?"

"The ides of progress. My building was ripped down on the approach to the bridge. Flower or your future?"

"I don't got money for either."

"The day is sweet. Indulge me." She held out her gnarled hand. "I do not bite."

When Mollie set her hand in Hermione's, she felt the tick of the old woman's pulse against her own. She saw the burgundy curtains flung to the street, the great wrecking ball smashing through the tenement, the set of tiny whiskey glasses shattered on the floor. Then there was again only her hand in the old woman's.

"Pick a card."

Mollie ran her fingers over the edges of the cards, felt the oil from so many hands. Then she pulled one from the arc.

"What is it?" Hermione asked.

"A wheel," Mollie said.

"The Wheel of Fortune. All of life contained within its circle: sadness and joy, cruelty and kindness, the future and the past. It stops for no one and nothing, for it is life itself. It may roll backwards to that you no longer wish to see, or forward to that you are terrified to know. It is your choice which way the wheel rolls. Pick another. Just one more."

Mollie crouched in front of Hermione.

"What is it?"

"Swords."

"How many?"

"Five."

"Ah, memory and fear. Five fears: betrayal, abandonment, ruin, joy, love. You hide behind walls to escape the fear that what hurt you once will hurt you again. But which is the fear that hurts you most?" Hermione coughed, deep and racking, and took a graying handkerchief from her waistband. Once the spasm subsided, she dabbed the edge of her lips.

"I ain't scared of nothing."

Hermione waved a hand in front of her eyes. "You don't have a coin or two to give an old lady?"

"I got nothing. I told you."

"Go now, and leave me to the sweet day. I'll trust you to bring me something, when you're of a mind to remember the entertainments of a mad old woman."

HESTER STREET

FRIDAY. ANYTHING YOU WANTED for any price you could pay. Potatoes, apples, and tin cups were piled nearly as high as the sky. Chickens and geese hung fat in windows. The aroma of fresh baked bread was thick. Fish of every sort, eyes blank pink-and-black, gazed at passersby. Planks of wood were set atop ash barrels, and overturned crates served as makeshift shops. At one stall alone, a person could buy cigars, hard lemon candy, sour milk edging from the top of metal pails, and a pair of (only) twice-mended socks.

Above the crowd that bought and sold, women leaned from windows and called to friends on the street. The sun had returned to the Lower East Side, and though the snow had melted and puddled between the cobblestones, no one minded it, because the light held such promise. The thought of spring made people slightly giddy: They laughed and bargained and strolled and daydreamed.

Though Mollie wanted to sit in the sun that angled across the cement, she chose instead the darker shadows. A safe place from which to watch.

Mollie knew she'd hurt Annabelle. She decided—since Annabelle continued to harp about reading—to pinch a book for her. Something simple, with small words and big letters.

A bookseller by the name of Schmidt had set up shop directly in front of Mollie's stoop. He puttered back and forth, arranging and rearranging, and muttering to himself. He was a squat man, in a cropped brown coat. His round glasses magnified his eyes, which made him seem both surprised and innocent at the same time.

"What time ya got?" Mollie asked him.

Schmidt pulled out a pocket watch and snapped open the case. He frowned, and then pushed his glasses up his nose, leaving a greasy thumbprint on the left lens. "Twenty past eleven. No—twenty-two past eleven." He closed the watch.

"Got any kid's books over there?"

"I might have. Let me see ..."

She'd let him point them out to her; she'd wait then for his back to be turned and she'd step up and take a book or two. Slide them into one of the long pockets of her coat. She thought she'd even smile at him as she departed.

A woman with kid gloves walked toward Schmidt's stand. She wore a dove-gray skirt and overcoat, both of fine wool, and held a basket filled with bread and flowers, which she set on a stack of books.

Mollie took a breath. It was that woman who had stolen all the bathtubs and replaced them with useless classes. It was the rich bitch who had asked Mollie if she was a good thief and then smirked when Mollie said she was. Well, it was time to show the woman a thing or two.

The woman pulled a sheaf of papers from under the

loaves. "May I leave flyers here?" she asked Schmidt. "New classes." A small silk change purse swung from her wrist as she handed him the papers.

"Miss DuPre." Schmidt bowed from his thick waist and peered around the thumbprint on his glasses. "I have the perfect book for you. *The Faerie Queen*. Spenser. I've saved it especially for you. There was a gentleman came by a moment ago wanting it, but I said, 'No. This book is reserved.'"

Miss DuPre laughed. "You'll make me poor with your books."

"Oh, I think not, Miss DuPre. And I'll set the flyers right here, up front for everyone to see."

Mollie stood and stretched. Oh, how nice her boots were, the soles soft enough that she felt the rounded cobblestones beneath her. Nice and quiet, too.

She reached into a special pocket she'd sewn near her waist and grasped her little knife. It would only take one slice—for the knife was very, very sharp—and a quick dash into the clamor of the butcher shop nearby. The purse looked heavy; there might be enough to take Annabelle out for a real feast. Maybe mutton or pudding or sherry. And God knows how soon Annabelle'd be needing three or *four* meals a day. There might even be enough for a whole box of books. That would certainly shut Annabelle up. And there'd certainly be enough for a few months' rent.

Mollie pulled the knife from her pocket, palming it so the blade wouldn't glint.

Down the steps she walked. Two steps. Three steps. A little bootblack slammed his case into her legs and she almost tumbled backwards. Any other time she would have taken a hand to the side of his head. But not now—no need to call attention.

She didn't pretend to look at the books—no one would think her a reader, anyway. She kept her eyes aimed toward the street, but that purse swung back and forth in the side of her vision. She passed the Do-Gooder—very close, close enough to smell the lemon verbena she wore. And oh, how the fabric draped so beautifully over the stupid rich woman's bustle. Mollie paused long enough to read the title of the book she held: *David Copperfield* by Charles Dickens. The pages were bordered by the yellow and brown of rot and age.

Mollie wouldn't pay a penny for something in such terrible condition. But here the woman was, opening her purse, so close to Mollie that the flutter it made in the air felt like fingers on her skin.

Still the woman did not notice her.

Mollie's blessing was that most people ignored her. This made for some of the easiest pickpocketing one could imagine. Even if the mark caught up with a policeman, even if he'd looked her right in the eyes, even if she'd bumped into the woman she'd pinched something from—why, when the policeman asked for a description, there were hems and haws and "I don't really remember"s. This allowed Mollie to wander merrily and innocently off from the scene, the goods she'd lifted already stashed in a pocket.

Mollie stood so close behind the woman, she could read those first lines:

Whether I shall turn out to be the hero of my own life, or whether that station will be held by anybody else, these pages must show.

She felt the heat of the woman's back, and noticed the sweat in the little pale tendrils of hair so carefully curled against her neck.

Schmidt gave a yellow-toothed smile. "And how is the settlement house, Miss DuPre?"

The woman straightened. "Very well. The baths are out, to make way for the children's room. You should come to an evening lecture."

A roar and bellow came from down the street. "*Thief!*"

Mollie turned her head toward the sausage stand, where a man in a black overcoat waved his hands and pointed down the street. A policeman's whistle shrieked. Mollie stifled a smile. She knew the cop's chase would be useless. A pickpocket could be a ghost when he wanted to be.

"It's education that will stop that. This is exactly why my settlement house will teach morals." Miss DuPre shook her head and returned to the books.

Mollie leaned in, then, turning the blade of her knife to the purse strings. It was a matter of half a second now.

"I wouldn't do that if I were you." Miss DuPre closed the book before her, and turned. She did not grab Mollie. She did not cry "thief." She pinned Mollie with a stare—not of disbelief, or fear, or anger—of challenge. There it was, flinting in the gold flecks of her pale eyes. As if she dared her to take the purse and suffer the consequences.

"I'm not doing nothing," Mollie said.

"You were about to take my purse."

"Now why would I want to do that?"

"I thought you were a good thief."

"Who said I was a thief? You saying I'm a thief? You know me? I ain't seen you in my life. I'm looking for a book. There ain't nothing wrong with that, is there?"

"Is the girl bothering you, miss?" Schmidt asked.

Emmeline DuPre flicked her hand, dismissing the bookseller as though he were nothing more than a bothersome gnat. Then she narrowed her eyes and murmured to Mollie, "Here. Take a flyer. There are better ways to do things than what you're doing."

Mollie glanced at it. Something about free lectures and classes.

"How's your friend?" Miss DuPre asked.

"You just accused me of trying to steal from ya, now you want to know about my friend?"

"She wants to read."

"And I want to be the queen of Egypt, but I'm busy doing other things. And so is she."

The Do-Gooder opened her mouth as if to speak, then set her lips in a thin line. She raised her arm toward Mollie, allowing the silk purse to dangle and sway. "Take it."

"What?"

"If you need the money, take the purse."

"You're nuts," Mollie said.

"Not enough of a challenge, is it?"

"I got no idea why you're talking to me." Mollie spun on her heel. She took a step forward, but was stopped by Miss DuPre's hand on her arm.

"I know exactly who you are."

"You don't know anything about me."

"I do."

"I'm gonna call for the police if you don't take your fucking hand off my arm."

The woman let go. She stepped back and took a deep breath. When she looked at Mollie again, there was no fierceness in her gaze, no set to her jaw. "I apologize."

"You oughtta."

She turned again to the books. "What were you looking for?"

"What?"

"You said you were looking for a book."

"Uh. Yeah. A kid's book. So's I can teach my friend."

Emmeline DuPre found an old primer, bought it, and gave it to Mollie. "Let me give you a tip. Don't watch your mark so long. I saw you coming a mile away."

Mollie did not know what to say. This do-gooder was quick enough to catch Mollie's game. She knew the definition of a mark and was sharp enough to keep herself from becoming one.

"Say thank you."

"For what?"

"The book."

"Thank you," Mollie managed.

Emmeline nodded and walked away.

When Mollie opened the cover, a thin piece of paper fluttered out. It was an advertisement for the brand-new Cherry Street Settlement House, with a list of classes and lectures for the month of March 1883.

OF RED CURLS

THEY FOUND HUGH AND Seamus loafing on the steps of Lefty Malone's. "Keeping a watch for the Rum Runners," Hugh said.

"Where's everyone else?" she asked. By which she meant Tommy, as she knew that Mugs was at his job at the butcher.

"Dunno." Hugh bounded down the steps, and grabbed an empty wooden box with a faded advertisement of big purple grapes and a woman in white holding a champagne flute. He flipped the box over and slid it so it bumped the rise.

"Don't mess with the box," Seamus said. "Lefty puts it there so's patrons think they're drinking *quality liquors*."

"I just need it for a minute. I want to show Mollie something." He sat on the lowest step, and pointed across the box. "Sit." He rolled his derby off his head; inside was a deck of cards. "Three-card draw."

"How do I know the deck ain't stacked?"

"Shuffle them yourself."

Mollie did. It was a new deck, and some of the cards stuck together. She bent the cards longways to loosen them.

Seamus picked up the *Police Gazette* from beside him and shook the pink pages open. "Careful there. Ya know how he don't like his cards messed with."

Mollie dealt. A pair of twos and a Jack. Too bad she didn't have a cent on her.

Hugh smacked his lips and smiled. "You staying?"

"Sure." She spread her cards before her.

"Not bad." Hugh rearranged his cards, each time lifting his shoulder and dropping it. "You got a twitch or something?"

"What? Little back trouble is all." Up and down went the shoulder. Then he stood and snapped his arm. "All I need's the queen of hearts, but I can't seem to shake her out of my sleeve." He rolled up his coat sleeve to show a metal contraption tied to his arm with leather straps. The queen of hearts was clamped to some spring-loaded thing. He shook his arm with more force, but the card wobbled and remained set in its mooring. "Aw, hell. She don't want to move." He sighed, then pulled the card free and kissed it. "You're a hard woman."

Mollie laughed. "How much you pay for that thing?"

"The fella said it worked like a dream. Even showed me. See, ya palm a queen before the deck's shuffled, and switch it out for a bum card. Then—*pow*—out comes the match, but only if you need it." Hugh wrangled with the spring on his arm, snapping and unsnapping it. "I got to get some oil. Hear how loud this is? I'd be dead before the card got in my hands. This thing's trash. I'm gonna find that fella and give him a chunk of my mind."

"*Piece* of my mind," Mollie said.

"Piece of lead would be better," Seamus added.

Hugh put his cards back in his hat and slapped it on his

head. He put his hands on his broad hips, flipping back the yellow-and-black-checked coattails, and gazed down the street. "Would ya look at that? Looks like we got a Jewboy who's very lost."

A young boy walked quickly down the opposite sidewalk, his eyes scraping the ground. He wore a broad hat rimmed with fur, and two large red curls swayed and bounced next to his cheeks.

"Hey Jewgirl," Hugh called. "How long's it take your mother to fix your hair? Meeting your boyfriend for a little rump-diddle-dee?"

The boy kept moving forward, his shoulders tight.

"Why don't ya answer me? Didn't no one teach you any manners?" Hugh checked both directions, and after a delivery van rolled by, crossed the street and stood directly in the middle of the sidewalk.

The boy stopped. He kept his eyes down. He stepped right. Hugh blocked him. He stepped left, but Hugh cut off that escape, too. Hugh's jacket blared in the sun. "Whatcha doing down here?"

"He's gonna shit his pants, he's so scared," Seamus said to Mollie.

"He's just walking."

Seamus handed the paper to her, then crossed the street.

The boy took a step backwards, bumping up against Seamus. Seamus pushed him forward with his chest, until he'd squeezed the kid between himself and Hugh.

"It's polite to answer questions," Seamus said. "So, whatcha doing down here?"

Hugh flipped the boy's curls. "Such a pretty little girl."

Then the boy took his chance, sliding from between them. He ran down the street, Seamus and Hugh on his heels.

Mollie chewed on her matchstick, chewed it until her teeth

ground the wood to pulp. Her stomach growled, nagging her yet again for food. She spit out the hard end of the match and swallowed the rest. She hoped the boy was fast.

When they returned, Seamus dangled a red curl in front of Mollie. "Like a souvenir?"

"What the hell did you do that for?"

Seamus's smile faltered. He looked at Hugh, then back at Mollie, his face puzzled. "What are you mad about?"

"What was the point? He wasn't doing nothing; he was walking down the street."

"He didn't answer me," Hugh said.

"Would *you* answer you?"

"What's your problem?" Seamus asked. "It wasn't like we beat him up or nothing. I cut a girly curl, is all. He should be thankful that's all I did. Jesus, Mollie, it was just fun."

"Where is he?" she asked.

"Long gone by now."

"Won't come back here, I bet," Hugh said.

"Did ya see him shake and chatter, Hugh?"

Click click click went Hugh's teeth.

"Well, did ya get his wallet, at least?" Mollie asked.

Seamus's dark eyebrows met. He blinked a few times. "I didn't think about it."

"So, you harassed the kid for absolutely no goddamn reason."

"I hate when you swear, Mollie."

Hugh waddled to the top step and sat down. "Don't know why you're so hot. It was fun." "Yeah, Mollie, it was fun." Seamus looked at the curl and tossed it into the gutter.

THE JOB

"SO, I'M TELLING ANNABELLE about how this Do-Gooder nearly caught my game. You know what she does? Yells at me. Tells me I'm taking money from people who is trying to improve themselves." She walked over to Seamus, who sat smoking on his bed, and turned so he could unhook the skirt.

"Then last week, she gets up when she hears the Italians stoking their stove—which is a god-awful time of morning—puts on her dress, her wig, and says, 'I'm going today.' That's it. And off she goes. Comes home at dinner and reads to me from this primer they gave her. *A is for Apple. B is for Bull-shit.* Gives me this look like she's better than me 'cause she's learning. *Improving* herself." Mollie pulled on a pair of moleskin trousers. She transferred her knife from her skirt to the back pocket of her trousers. "Don't talk to me at all besides that. Just reads and reads all morning. Tells me to *shut up* if you can believe that. Then she puts on her paint and goes out on the street for about fifteen minutes. Comes back in saying there ain't any johns worth her while. Goddamn stubborn—"

"That Do-Gooder's gotta be paying off a lot of people. Fucking Protestant. Somebody should have burned the place down by now."

"And you know what else she says? 'I'll teach people to dream.'"

"Annabelle?"

"The Do-Gooder."

"Dreams, huh? I got plenty of those. Don't need someone to teach me how to do it." "Like what?"

Seamus shrugged and ran a hand through his hair. "I dunno. I'd like my own dancehall. Better than Lefty's. With girls who can actually dance. What about you?"

"Brooklyn."

"Oh, yeah. That."

Mollie yanked back her hair and knotted it into a bun. "What time is it?"

"I dunno. I got my watch nipped yesterday," Seamus said.

"Idiot."

"Maybe *you* took it."

"I ain't seen ya in a week."

"Really?"

"Really."

"Guess it wasn't you. Maybe another pretty girl got it."

She sat beside him, unbuttoning her blouse. He slid the fabric down her shoulders and gave her that cockeyed smile that had always made her heart thump and flutter. "Not now. I gotta focus."

"You're beautiful."

"And you ain't listening. I'm telling you about Annabelle. Give me that shirt."

He handed her a soft white shirt that lay folded on the bed; she pulled it quickly over her head. "What's the plan?"

Seamus snuffed his cigarette. "All you gotta know is your part. We're gonna hoist you through the transom window at the back door. Watchman'll be sitting at a little table nearby. Get the keys, walk straight forward to the front door. Unlock it, step out, whistle diddly-dee-dee and move along on your way. I'll have your dress in the alley two doors over, near the Anchor."

"What's the rest? What's the take?"

"Never you mind, Mollie. Let's just say payday's tomorrow and there's a load of cash in the safe. Maybe you and me can go take a carriage round the park next week."

"How much is the take, Seamus?"

"Tommy didn't say. Just said it's a lot."

"That's so he can take a bigger cut without you being the wiser."

"It's so's if one of us gets caught, no one else is the wiser. You know that."

Mollie stood and stared at herself in the mirror above Seamus's chest of drawers. In the tight trousers and shirt, she looked very much like a boy, like any of the thousands of boys who roamed the streets. "Thank God you got a brother who's got clothes that fit me. Imagine me crawling through a transom window in petticoats."

Buttery soft fingers. Buttery soft shoes. A foot in Mugs's thick hand, a boost to the window. She placed her hands on his shoulders and maneuvered so her feet entered through the window first.

"Good luck, Moll."

"See you at your ma's for a late dinner?" she whispered.

"Corned beef and beer."

She let go a hand, felt for the top frame of the door, and held on. Let go the other. Dropped to the floor inside.

Crossed herself. Breathed. Waited for the sounds of the rigging warehouse, the creaks of tarred rope, the echoes and sighs of the high ceiling, to become as familiar as her own breath. Let her eyes adjust, for there was only a single gaslight spitting near the middle of the room. One small square table below it. One man with his head in his arms, snoring.

Damn. Too bad he wasn't a drunk who sprawled, leaving his pockets open for God and all to see.

She stepped into the shadows, moving slowly toward him. Where would he keep the key? A front pocket near the thigh would be obvious. A good watchman, even a drunk good watch-man, would tuck the key in a pocket near his chest. Near a chest, Mollie saw, that bore the weight of him.

A is for Apple. B is for Burglary. C is for Caught. No—Cat. Shit.

She watched the edge of the man's gray mustache flip up and settle down. He was nowhere near close to changing position. And by the empty brown bottle on the table, he was also very drunk.

Who are you stealing from, Mollie Flynn? Thought you had some morals. Stealing the pay from those who don't make much more than you and me.

Annabelle's words, in the voice of the Do-Gooder.

Mollie shook her head. Why in the hell did she hear Emmeline DuPre? Where was the hum, the flattening of sound?

This man, whose cheeks were scarred with the hard veins of drink, would—once the robbery was complete—most certainly lose his job. This man, whose heavy, thick hands showed him too old for much other employment, might have babies at home or at least a wife.

Mollie stepped closer, into the circle of gaslight now. Well, if he wasn't a low drunk, this wouldn't happen at all.

Yes, that thought worked.

And it wasn't her concern what happened to him, was it? Her concern was paying off the debt. Her concern was getting enough money for her and Annabelle to cross the bridge to Brooklyn and trees and sky and being good for once in their goddamn lives.

Too bad for him. There were consequences to everything.

She stood behind him. She reached across his chest. Slid a buttery soft finger under the rough wool. There was the edge of the pocket. The warm heat of a key ring.

Then it happened. A roll and rumble in her stomach, a gurgle of hunger that echoed between the rolls of rope. Something that had no place in here. He might have slept to the crack and blister of tarred ropes, to his own snores, but not this. Not this sound that was only a hungry stomach, and not his own.

The watchman jerked his head back, and Mollie came face-to-face with his gray lips and wine-red veins. Her fingers still touched the ring of keys.

If I'm still, he'll think I'm a dream.

He reached up a hand, clamping down on her wrist. Twisted round to see her better. With his free hand, he fumbled toward his coat pocket. Looking for a knife or slungshot, or worse, a gun. Holding her, holding her right near him and damn if his fingers did not dig deep.

Mollie pulled her eyes from him long enough to spy the front door. Fifty feet if not more. And even there, she'd have no way out, not without the key still teasing at her grasp.

Damn Tommy. Damn him for this.

One hand fishing out the key ring. The other loose and searching. Then the bottle was in her hand (how had it got there?) and a *thunk* as it hit bone. Gray skin blossomed crimson.

She was loose, now, for the watchman put his palms to his forehead. He bellowed and rocked in his seat. She ran across the space, feeling the keys, hoping she could find the one that fit the lock, turned the tumblers, and released her to the night.

His steps were behind her, not clipping, but sagging and drunk and slightly off course.

Which key, which key? *Look at the lock, Mollie, you've done this plenty of times before.* She opened her palm, checked the shapes of the keys. Matched them to the lock, and felt the tumble and release.

He was behind her, now. She dropped the keys, put both hands on the doorknob, and pulled.

Straight to the street then, though the whistle the watchman blew rang in her ears and the bell he clanged echoed against her back. The fish were in; the air smelled fuggy. She took a breath anyway, and knew not to run. Walk like a boy looking for his girl or a prostitute. Put your hands in your pockets and never mind there's blood that sticks.

Where were the boys? They'd be in alleyways, behind barrels, in doorways. She needed them now. Before the bell and the whistle roused the waterfront police.

A dark shape drew from a row of barrels, a head bare of a hat, a flapping collar. Thank God. Seamus. Maybe he'd jump the watchman and shut him up.

But then came a pop, dry, hot, and savage.

The pop of a gun. No more bell, just the tripping clink of a metal whistle against stone. She turned her head. The watchman lay dead on the street.

And the white collar flapped as Seamus darted away.

Another alley and she'd find her skirt and blouse and no one would blame her for anything.

The cobblestones were slick with drizzle. Ships on the left, buildings on the right. *Find the alley, don't get blinded by the saloon doorway light.* Laughter rolled from cracked windows and tripped her.

Other footsteps, heavy and hard, came near, slowing at the body, then loping forward.

One step, two steps, three to the alley and her own clothes.

She slid through the narrow gap of the buildings, dropping to her knees and fumbling for the bundle that would make her once again innocent.

There. She ripped off the shirt, grabbing her own. God, her hands couldn't catch the buttons. It didn't matter. Pull off the trousers and pull up the skirts, fasten the waist. Breathe. Her fingers tore at her hair, setting it free from the tight bun. She shook her head. She needed to leave the alley looking like nothing more than a prostitute.

One step, two steps, three to gain the street. She noticed two blues bending over the watchman's body. A sleek figure sauntered slowly by them, unhurried and not a bit curious. He continued to walk, a cigarette between his perfect lips. As he passed her, he slowed, shook his head, and flicked the cigarette near her feet. Then he brushed the lapels of his jacket, pulled the sleeves to lose the wrinkles, and continued on. He didn't catch her gaze. When Tommy McCormack was disappointed in someone, he ignored them. And left them to swing whichever way the wind decided to blow.

If only she could focus. Should she walk toward the body, as if she'd just come upon it? Or away, like she hadn't noticed? Jesus, the watchman probably had a wife. *It's not human anymore—nothing you can do about it. You didn't ask Seamus to pull a trigger. You didn't want to hear the dry pop of a bullet. You only wanted to run.*

Away. Get away. Put your back to it all and go home. Help Annabelle with her lessons. Sit in the glow of candlelight and pretend.

RAIN

WHAT HAVE YOU DONE, Mollie Flynn?

Move your feet. It's raining. The raindrops bounce off the cobblestones like so many tears. Can't see the river for the ships. The masts sway. They look like crosses, or grave markers. So thin and naked they might break in two. *Don't stand in the rain—you're a daft bitch to do so. Look, you're soaked through.*

Step into the shadows, Mollie. There's sailors coming by. No one notices you; you're a good little thief.

Mollie can't feel her feet and hands; she waits for the rest of her to go numb, too.

The rain is thick like frosted glass. The water slides in sheets to the river. Steam rises from the decks of the ships.

Go home, Mollie, someone's waiting for you. There's a stove and heat. You can lock the door and never come out. You can tell Annabelle Lee she was right to be superstitious.

It's gray now, on the river. It's night still, on the street. Watch the sky lighten and the shadow darken the doorway you stand in. Stop shaking—you didn't shoot the gun.

Look, Mollie, beyond the ships. Look at the stones, look at the arches and cables, look how the top of the tower is hidden in fog. So much bigger than the pictures. Taller than anything you've ever seen. Look at the stevedores, coming to work. They walk past the bridge; they ignore it. They're here to load the ships and send them coursing. They walk past you, Mollie. Hold your breath and pray they ignore you, too.

"Get out of the doorway, miss."

The rain is sharp, but it does not clean.

There's people before you, Mollie. Don't bump into them. There are carts coming toward you. The stevedore with the broad-brimmed hat says something; his mouth opens and closes like a fish. His eyes are kind. What's he saying? There's nothing to hear but the rain. What's he saying? He's asking her a question. He's set his cart down. He's waiting for an answer.

Mollie opens her mouth and screams. Mollie walks past him and keeps screaming. It's the only thing blocking the roar of the rain and there's too many drops to count now. One block, two blocks. There's the Elevated, leaving the station. She sees the lights inside and the dark figures of people pushing in. When it leaves, the ground shudders beneath her; the train itself is swallowed by water and all the people inside will drown.

Look how no one stops you, Mollie Flynn. You can scream your head off and no one does a thing about it. But then the water parts like a curtain, and out comes a long blue coat and a badge. He wants you to stop screaming, Mollie. He'll take you to the station house if you don't shut up.

Run, Mollie. If you don't, you'll drown.

The mud sucked and pulled at Mollie's feet as she crossed the yard. The rain coursed down, each heavy drop reflecting the orange glow of the tenement windows. She stepped into the rookery's hallway, which smelled already of mold.

"Yer wet." Little Ian played marbles on the floor. A yellow light slashed from the partially open door to his apartment. Behind it, Mollie saw his mother. She held a pot. "Mam says you can die if yer out in the rain when you shouldn't be." Ian flicked a marble that passed near Mollie's shoe. "Maybe yer dead now."

She tried to fit the key in the lock, but her hand shook too much. She knocked. The door flew open. Annabelle stood in front of her; Annabelle crushed her in her arms.

"Oh, Mollie."

There was someone else, then, pushing past Annabelle. Seamus? Yes, Seamus. He pulled her against him, kissing the top of her head.

"Don't touch me." She scratched at his face and hit him in the chest. He let her go.

She saw the boys, then. They all stood smashed together in the tiny room: Hugh and Mugs on the bed, Tommy standing by the table.

Annabelle slowly raised a hand to Mollie's cheek. "You're so cold." She turned and yanked the blanket from the mattress, pulling it out from under Hugh and Mugs. "Get off the bed."

Mollie felt the weight of wool, but did not find its heat.

It was very bright. The kerosene lamp they used on special occasions burned white. There was something else on the table, something she'd never seen there before: guns. She counted them, because she could not take the looks in the boys' eyes—the questioning and silence. *One, two, three, four. One, two, three—*

"We looked for you at the police station, Mollie." Seamus put out a hand to touch her, then thought better of it. "Mugs and Hugh went up to the Tombs for six-o'clock court. Me and Tommy checked the streets, we checked every alley we could think of, and we couldn't find you." His voice broke. He dabbed his handkerchief against the scratch Mollie'd made on his cheek.

"We thought you'd been tapped," Hugh said. "The police, they was everywhere last night."

One, two, three steps—

"Go get some whiskey from across the street." Tommy peeled off bills from a roll and handed them to Mugs.

"Get out." Mollie's voice was no more than a breath. "Get—" Mollie's eyes caught Seamus's. His lips were white. He had pulled the trigger that shot the bullet that killed a man. All because of her. There are consequences to everything. "—out."

Tommy nodded. The boys each picked up a gun: *one, two, three, four.*

Annabelle unbuttoned Mollie's shirt and peeled it from her shoulders. She laid it over the table to dry. She lifted Mollie's arms, pulled off her chemise. She dipped a rag in water warmed on the stove and ran it across Mollie's back, down her legs, and up the inside. She braided Mollie's hair. Over and over, Annabelle dipped the rag in the water and washed Mollie's skin clean. An arm, a foot, a cheek.

Annabelle did not talk because there was no need for it. She did not talk, and Mollie was grateful.

She gave Mollie her nightdress. She sat her on the edge of the bed and handed her a plate with two biscuits.

"I'm not hungry."

"You need to eat." Annabelle broke off a piece of the biscuit and held it to Mollie's lips. "Please."

The bread caught in her throat, and she coughed, sending crumbs flying. Annabelle poured her a glass of gin. She took a swallow. She asked for another glass. She waited for the numbness.

"What happened?"

"Got a man killed. Seamus tell you that?"

"Oh, Moll."

"I steal. I don't want no part of killing," Mollie said. The room looked as if it were underwater: The stove floated, the table bobbed up and down, Annabelle's dresses swam like beautiful fish.

"I've never seen you cry," Annabelle said.

"That what I'm doing?"

"Seamus had to do it. The man knew what you looked like. Didn't he?"

Mollie pushed the heels of her hands into her eye sockets until she saw only blue and silver stars.

Mollie stayed in the bed. The only time she left was to visit the outhouse. In the yard, the water rose from all the rain; bottles and cans and papers floated on the dirty skin of it. Some of the outhouses flooded, and their stench rose like a thick gas.

Seamus had come by. She had not answered the door. He had stood outside for hours, then finally given up. Sometimes it was so quiet, Mollie heard the Italians sewing buttonholes next door. Annabelle went out each day. Each night—very late—the lock would tumble, and the door would click and squeal against its hinges. Annabelle would drop coins on the table, then take off her wig and hang it on a hook. She pulled at the pins that held her hair, and let it tumble over her shoulders. She loosened her stays, letting out a great sigh.

She wandered from task to task: a bit of coal pushed around in the stove to get the last of its heat, candlewicks trimmed and lit and placed on the table, the dress removed and shaken out and hung up. She would wash herself then, scrubbing every bit of her body, shivering at the wet rag.

"Not many biting today," she'd say. "And those who do ain't worth the coins."

Or "Mugs sent along some meat. I think I'll make stew—that'll get you up again. We ain't had stew in ages. Course that's because we both hate it."

Or "Maybe you can show me how to work a pen without getting ink all over my hand. Look like I got some disease. Would you help me, Moll?"

And then, one night, when her lip was split and swollen, she yanked Mollie from the bed. "Get up. I can't trick anymore. It hurts. All right?"

"Who gave you the lip?"

"We need money."

"Who gave you the lip, Annabelle?"

"Tommy. Who else? I told him the baby was his. But you were right, weren't you? He don't give fuck-all—"

"I'm gonna kill that son of a bitch."

"He promised me he'd settle for ten dollars."

"Before or after he hit you?" Mollie asked.

"We need money."

"But I did that sneak thief. He said he'd forgive the whole thing."

Annabelle pointed to the tin box on the shelf over the bed. "There's six dollars and thirteen cents in there. That's all we got. I'm pregnant, Moll. I need you. And I need ya to not be dead."

DELANCEY

MOLLIE STARED AT THE door. She took a breath. Turned the kerosene switch until the flame went blue, then snuffed black. She stood in the dark, before the door, and crossed herself.

The small window at the end of the hall thumped against the rotten frame. It was the wind, playing with the glass. Shrieks of laughter and a boy's howl came from the yard below.

She approached the window, opening it enough to look down past the outhouse roofs. The cool air felt sharp against her skin, and she pulled her hands back, crossing her arms.

Three little boys had claimed the muddy stretch of land between the tenements and made it their kingdom. Two of the boys were at the age when legs and arms gained confidence, and each day they challenged their bodies to throw stones just a little farther, jump higher on the mountain of garbage that bulged and balanced at a threatening height. The third boy Mollie recognized as Ian, the little boy from the first floor. He trailed along behind the other two, and the stones he threw at the cans the boys had set atop the outhouses never made their mark. Still, he did not complain, even when the other two tripped him for no reason but their own amusement, or pulled his hair, or jumped from the outhouses to scare him.

The boys played ferociously on their mountain, throwing each other off, rolling down, and climbing back up. The tallest one reached the very pinnacle; he crouched down, opened the top trash bag, and rummaged around. He removed cans and bottles, stacking them on the brick window ledge of a second-story room.

"I own this mound," he said, "and I'll knock the head off anyone who tries to take it."

This was of course not a warning to his friends, but an invitation readily accepted. Ian stared at the ground, as if pondering a strategy. But the other boy leaped up, his red hair like flame. The king of the pinnacle would not be removed. The redhead received quite a wallop from a can. It didn't matter. Up he immediately climbed again, a full frontal assault. The king dug again in the bags. He threw whatever his hands found available, which meant chicken bones, a rotten cabbage, a piece of bread hard as rock.

While the boys fought, Mollie watched Ian pick his way slowly up the side of the garbage mountain. He did not look up at his quarry, nor did he make the mistake of looking down at the ground. He climbed up and up. What would happen at the top? The bigger boy would shove Ian off completely, and laugh in triumph. Might makes right.

It was the way of the Fourth Ward.

Down the stairs. A hand running along the wall from habit, from darkness, from the lack of a railing to keep one's balance. Pass the yard, pass the boys, pass the mothers churning laundry. Slip through the narrow alley. Claim the street. *Walk it like you've done before, Mollie.*

But Lord, how the people passed so close, jarring her shoulder, darting in front of her, coming up from behind—she watched and walked. She needed a mark. One good mark. Someone who kept their money with them. Someone like Maud Riley, who had a vegetable stand and collected money all day.

Her chest was tight. What the hell was she thinking? Maud Riley knew her. Maud Riley'd tap her in a second and turn her over to the cops.

Noise tumbled around her, and she knew there was nothing for her to do but continue to walk and think. Watch out for Tommy or the boys. *Take a breath: It's only four dollars you need.* Rent would be tomorrow's problem.

Water dripped from windowsills and awnings, and pooled under the tables of vegetables at the grocer's. Horses churned up mud from beneath the cobblestones. The air was filled with dampness that steamed from the sidewalk, from wool coats, from the stone and brick buildings. She looked up at the telegraph wires crisscrossing the sky like a spider's web. Holding her in. Holding her to this life.

"Watch out!" Someone put a hand on her arm and moved her from the path of a huge pushcart filled with furniture.

"Don't touch me." She jerked her arm away. "Don't ever touch me."

The man who stopped her gestured to the cart. "You were going to walk right—"

"Then let me walk into it. It's got nothing to do with you if I do or don't."

"Got a mouth on you, don't you?" He ambled away, shaking his head.

At the livery stable, two horses waited in their tracings and blinders, nodding off in the steamy sun. Their whole lives, good or bad or indifferent, were entirely up to the whim of their owner. Did they ever wish for something else?

She crossed Batavia, walking along Roosevelt. The tenements all blended together, stoop after stoop, brick facades covered in black dirt, some buildings with new fire escapes—or easy entries, as the boys had pointed out. In between the flat stones of the sidewalk, Mollie saw the bright green of newly sprung grass. In a matter of days, it would all be trampled and brown. Yet, there it was, every year, just the same, beautiful and so fragile it made Mollie want to cry.

Do the only thing you know how to do, Mollie Flynn. The grass is just grass and you didn't shoot the gun. It's not guilt burning your gullet. It's fear.

She wandered up and down Delancey for hours. The clouds were lumpy, heavy with bad temper, and the air, swollen and still, was tinged with a strange emerald light. Soon it would rain.

It should have been easy, finding marks on this wide, busy street, what with all the people getting off the streetcars with empty hands, then returning with arms full of packages. It should have been easy when the fire-truck bell clanged and everyone shaded their eyes to watch the horses galloping by. And then there was the emporium with flour and salt and ready-made collars and bolts of fabric and not one eye on her. So many opportunities.

Yet, each time she stepped in closer to a fat wallet or a carelessly held purse, she could not complete the take. Where was the flattening of sound, the narrowing of focus? Mollie's head ached—filled with all the sounds of the streets, all the back-and-forth movement of the people. And how her hands shook! She barely escaped touching the fingers of a woman who had reached in her purse for a handkerchief.

Googs Mallory had told her once: "Five seconds of thinking

is three seconds too long." And here Mollie had stood like a moron from Bellevue, letting the minutes go by.

"Goddammit," she said out loud. She stuck a match in her mouth and trudged back to the corner where she began. She leaned against a green iron railing. The sign above advertised THE FINEST CHAIRS IN NEW YORK. THIRD FLOOR. The windows behind her contained photographs of scowling couples, and a few stills of some actress in tights and a very short skirt that barely came to her knees.

On the corner, shaded by the awning of a café entrance—a café, for God's sake!—a policeman stood watch, his arms crossed. His mustache was well oiled. The badge on his chest gleamed. He looked at Mollie and she looked at him.

"All right already, I'm leaving." She pushed away from the railing and sashayed by him.

She bought a hot wine from a pushcart. She dropped the change. She used both hands to keep the cup steady. *Jesus Christ*, she thought. *What the hell am I gonna do now*?

Mollie thought she might ride the streetcar back and forth; whoever sat by her would have bad luck that day. She would have liked to rest her feet, anyway. She crossed the middle of the street, and clambered up the stairs. She stood near the door—just in case she'd need to get out fast. A plump woman in plain black squeezed next to her. The condensed moisture of everyone's breath fogged the windows. The vehicle jolted forward. Mollie fell into the woman. This was quite a good thing, for her leg bumped something that felt very much like a bag of coins and bills.

The woman held a large knit bag on her lap, and the joints of her hands were white from holding it so tight. Another stop, another clatter and lunge. Mollie put her hand on the bench to right herself and left it there. Let the weight of it against the smooth wood seat still, for one second, the shaking. Let her fingers move slowly, feeling the fabric for the opening. Feeling for the thicker seam. There.

She felt sorry for this woman. This woman thought herself so smart, pretending to guard money in her big knit bag, thinking no one would look elsewhere. Or perhaps she had something in the bag she didn't want to lose. Mollie thought it might be food and she might be going home to a large family of boys who would eat it all and leave her only the scraps and gristle. The woman blinked a lot, as if the diffused light that somehow made its way through the windows was too bright. She smelled of coffee and years of boiled meat and something flowery meant to hide the first two smells. Mollie hesitated. She removed her hand and instead smoothed and repinned her bun. At the next stop, the woman got off, and it was then the sound slipped to nothing but the pump of Mollie's heart.

It should have been easy; it would have been, had the damn woman not turned on a side street, had the crowd not thinned to nothing, had the woman not spun directly around to smack Mollie in the head with her bag.

Mollie could have run away. Mollie could have called the cops.

But she shoved the woman into an alley, then to the ground, and held her sharp knife to the woman's throat. She took the money from her pocket.

She pushed the tip of the blade into soft skin—just a bit—and the woman started to cry. "Are you scared?" Mollie whispered. A barge whistle blew. The river was close.

Jesus. There was a knife in her hand, held to a woman's throat, and the woman was crying.

What have you become, Mollie Flynn?

She stepped back, dropped the knife, and ran.

CHERRY STREET SETTLEMENT HOUSE

ONE BUILDING STOOD OUT from the others. The brick was blustery red, the long windows of its three stories shimmering and bright. The awning was striped in green and white. The steps had been replaced; the columns of the portico had been stripped of plaster, and the original marble showed its veins. It looked very much like the new kid in the yard who was sure to be beaten up. Mollie felt a momentary sense of displacement. Where was she now? It should have been Cherry Street directly ahead; that building should be the baths. There should be a broken streetlamp fast by the entrance, not a new glass globe and freshly painted pole.

She squinted—yes, just faintly the word BATH could be made out on the brick. The only other sign was quite small, as if the building did not really wish to advertise itself. It was a rectangle of brass, just to the right of a door that no longer had wood planks across its bottom: CHERRY STREET SETTLEMENT HOUSE.

A group of women and men, all with the rough hands and sallow cheeks that identified them immediately as belonging to the Fourth Ward, loitered near the door or stepped inside.

Mollie glanced at Annabelle. She barely recognized her. She did not wear her blonde wig, nor any paint. She held a slim book in her hands, and her face was open and bright. Mollie suddenly remembered the moldy curled pages of Dickens. What was the first line she'd so carelessly read that day so long ago? *Whether I shall be the hero of my own life ...* and something else.

It was all so far away from Mollie, though only twenty steps or so to cross the street and climb the stairs.

Annabelle took her hand. "Come on, ya daft bitch. No one bites."

Nothing at all about the vestibule—where they had once come to sign in and bathe—looked the same, except for the stained glass of Jesus and the lambs. In place of the matron at the desk, and the pail where girls dropped their coins, stood a tall counter. Behind it, a large woman with pince-nez, a white shirt, and starched collar and tie, watched as both women and men signed in.

"Never seen a woman in a tie before," Mollie whispered to Annabelle.

"It's the matron from the baths, Moll. She's still a dragon."

Behind the counter, a large sign read:

NO SWEARING
NO RUNNING
NO GAMBLING
NO DRINKING
NO KNIVES OR GUNS

The matron set a different ledger before Mollie. "Name, address, and time checked in. You'll wait here for an interview."

"An interview? Why?"

"The rules are the rules."

The gaslights hummed; they were not needed, for the room was painted so white that Mollie wanted to shade her eyes. She dipped the pen in the ink bottle, but then her hand twitched, and the ink splattered across the paper.

"I got a problem with my hands," Mollie muttered. She felt Annabelle rub her back.

The matron cleared her throat and raised her eyebrows. She waited for Mollie's name.

Yes, Mollie thought. *I can do this. I signed my name many times before.* She placed the pen against the paper.

"Your real name," the matron said. "Your real address."

"All right already."

Mollie Flynn. 32 Oak Street. 510C.

The head matron plucked the pen from her hand. She read Mollie's name, then slid the pad aside and pushed the other in place. She handed the pen to Annabelle. "Come, come, come."

"She can't write," Mollie said. "I'll sign for her."

"No, Mollie. I can do it myself."

And there Annabelle stood, biting her lip, signing her very own name.

"Well, I'll be damned," Mollie said.

The matron raised a thick finger to the List of Rules. "No swearing."

"Did I swear?" Mollie said innocently as they moved away from the counter.

Annabelle kissed her cheek. "I'm late. And I can't run."

"'Cause of the rules."

"'Cause I'm suddenly big as a house." Her eyes flicked

behind her. A man in a drab suit signed his name, then stuck his fingers back in his vest and turned to look at them. He had a long nose and chin, and his hair was oiled tight to his head and colorless as his clothes. His jacket sagged where his shoulders should have filled it out, and his pants hung as if they were made for someone else. But it was as if he thought himself as finely dressed as a Broadway gent, for he rocked back on his heels, smiled at Mollie, then sauntered down the hall.

The matron clucked, and pointed to a long bench. "You'll wait there for Miss DuPre."

Mollie sank down, and almost slid off the polished wood.

She grasped the edge with her fingers, as much to keep her balance as to keep them still.

The stairs that once led to the baths were filled with rolling and tumbling children. Their mothers waved to them from the main floor, and there were thrown kisses, and sullen glares from kids not wanting to go up. The matron looked at the round clock above Mollie's head, then clapped and shushed the children up the stairs.

Shrieks and laughter came from the old bath floor. The hallway beyond the counter echoed with "good morning"s. Then a bell sounded, and quiet came. So much quiet that Mollie heard only the tick of the clock and the scratch of the matron's pen.

Outside, carts and carriages rolled by. A woman dragged a wheeled cart filled with fabric. A prostitute and her john exited the alley directly across the street and went their separate ways.

A sharp click of heels echoed from the hallway. Emmeline DuPre held the edge of a door in each hand, and shut them to the classrooms beyond. She approached the matron. "Did Terence come?"

"No, miss. Looked for him especially."

"Hmm."

Miss DuPre wore an ivory dress. She pushed her thin wire-rim glasses up her nose and read through the names of those who had signed in. "Not bad. And new students?"

And new? Mollie rolled her eyes. *There ain't no one but me sitting like a fool on this bench,* she wanted to say. Instead, she whistled a bit of a tune from the dancehall, until Miss DuPre looked at her over the top of her glasses.

"Add 'No Whistling' to the list," she said to the matron. "Come," she said to Mollie. She picked up her skirts and ascended the stairs. She did not turn and make sure Mollie followed; she knew Mollie followed.

They passed the second floor and the thumps and bumps of the children. The third floor appeared to be a sort of dormitory. It was all so white.

"I'll furnish those rooms this summer. Perhaps you and Miss Lee would—"

"We got our own place, thank you."

The stairs now narrowed sharply and grew steeper. At the top were two doors. Three locks separated the right door from whatever lay behind it. Miss DuPre turned the knob on the left door.

Tall oak cabinets lined three walls of the small, plain room. The fourth wall was mostly window, with lace curtains softening the light. A great desk with carved feet took up most of the space. Two horsehair chairs angled in front of it. The top of the desk was covered in stacks of paper, each stack held down by a book. A pipe hung from the ceiling, with two closed gas jets attached to each end. There were no paintings on the wall, no pictures on the cabinets. Only the paint that still smelled of lead and turpentine.

Emmeline DuPre perched on the corner of her desk and gestured to a seat. "Please."

Mollie sat. The fabric, when her hands found it, was thick. It was not a chair, once settled in, that one could easily run from.

Miss DuPre moved behind the desk and sat. The springs in the chair creaked. "Can you read?"

"Yes."

"Were the rules understandable?"

"Yes."

"How old are you?"

"Sixteen. I think."

"I'm thirty-seven. I know. So. Classes begin at eight and let out at four. There is an hour break for lunch. Two hours a day, each student must work at a job around the facility."

"A job?"

"A job. Painting, cleaning, watching the children on the playground. Cleaning the blackboards. This is not a charity."

"Annabelle's been working?" "Miss Lee watches the children from ten to twelve. Why are you laughing?"

Mollie bit her lip. "I'm not laughing."

"She's learning how to care for them."

"I hope she ain't teaching them anything."

"You, Miss Flynn, have no faith in your friend. And she knows it."

"What are you talking about? I got great faith in Annabelle. Don't tell me how I am with Annabelle."

The Do-Gooder's face remained clear and blank. "Why are you here?"

"I want you to fix my hands. Look at 'em."

Emmeline DuPre leaned back in her chair and tapped a finger against her lips. "A pickpocket with bad hands. Hmm."

"I ain't going through this again. I wasn't gonna steal your purse."

"What do you want from your life?"

"What do you mean?"

"Do you want to pickpocket again? Do you want to be the best thief in New York City?"

Mollie saw the watchman lying in the street, saw herself holding a sharp knife to a woman's throat. "I just need my hands to be still. That's all I'm asking."

"What then?"

"You wouldn't understand."

Miss DuPre held Mollie's gaze. "Try me."

"You just wouldn't, all right? You got no idea—"

"Don't underestimate me, Miss Flynn."

"Don't underestimate *me*."

"Which means?"

"I can be good. Whatever you think."

"So we'll see." Miss DuPre opened a desk drawer. "This is the contract everyone must sign. Basically, you agree to the rules, you agree to the work, you agree to learn a trade." She handed the paper to Mollie.

"Says near the bottom that if the rules are broken, you're not allowed back."

"That's correct."

"What if you break them on your own time?"

"That's of no concern to me."

"You got a pen?"

Miss DuPre handed her one. Not the kind that one dipped in ink, but a new one with its own mechanism and bladder, and scrolls of gold.

"Nice pen." And again, Mollie Flynn signed her real name. She blew on the ink to dry it. "So what class am I taking?"

"Typewriting. It's a new field, and there are jobs open for women."

"How much does it pay?" Mollie asked. "When you've got your typewriting degree or whatever it is."

"Three dollars a week."

"How many hours a day?"

"Twelve hours, Sundays off."

"Twelve hours a day." Mollie shook her head. "That's not bad." *Unless you're a pickpocket who works when she wants and can make three dollars in a heartbeat.* At least if the day was lucky and your hands were still.

The Do-Gooder stood; Mollie followed. They shook hands.

"That's all, then. I'll escort you to your class. You're lucky. We've just started on the home-row letters."

Miss DuPre opened the door. She again led the way, stopping only for Mollie to exit the office. She closed the door behind her. She did not lock it.

Mollie pointed to the three locks on the facing door. "So what's behind there?"

The Do-Gooder was already half a flight down from her. "My home."

"You live here?"

"Someday I'll tell you my story. I like this neighborhood."

"Jesus."

"And I'd like my pen, Miss Flynn."

ASDF JKL;

THE CLATTER AND CLACK of typewriters ricocheted around the hall, sounding a lot, Mollie realized, like the pop of pistols. It took all her strength not to run. Emmeline DuPre guided her through the door; the typewriting slowed and stopped. The room was perfectly square, with dark square desks. Upon each surface sat a black metal typewriter and above each set of keys labored a set of hands. Twenty pairs of eyes moved from the great chalkboard that held the drill to be practiced. Twenty pairs of eyes examined Mollie Flynn.

The women were dressed in all they could afford, grays and browns that had been repaired many times. The men kept their coats on, and some were collarless. One woman up front looked Mollie over and gave a small, disapproving cough.

"Good morning," Miss DuPre said to the class.

"Good morning," they murmured in unison. Little worker-bees under the spell of a beautiful do-gooder.

The Do-Gooder stepped over to the teacher. He was a tall man, with white hair growing from his ears. His glasses, on a chain, lay against his chest. His vest and coat were black. He stood with his hands clasped behind his back. He had very large feet. He bent to hear Miss DuPre's soft words and nodded. He pointed to an empty desk in the front row.

Not there, Mollie thought. She ignored the curious faces, and spied another seat in the back corner. That was the seat she needed. The man who'd smiled at her in the vestibule not an hour before waved from the desk right next to it.

Miss DuPre turned to Mollie, gesturing at the typewriter in the front row. "Take a seat, Miss Flynn."

"I want to sit back there."

"Very well. As long as you sit, so the class may continue."

Mollie held her skirt tight to her and squeezed through the row, with everyone watching.

The long-chinned man leaned over to her. "Never mind Miss Witch up front. She only approves of herself. I'm Charlie White, by the way."

She did not answer him, but stretched her legs under the desk and marveled at the strange machine in front of her.

Place the paper, turn the roller. Hold your hands high over the home row: ASDFJKL; press firmly, and watch the silver keys in front of you tap blurry black letters on the white paper. Thumb goes to the space bar. Do not look at the keys; follow the drill on the chalkboard. Hope the teacher's long, black-clad legs do not choose to stop in front of you. That he does not push his glasses up his nose and roll the paper out of the machine.

"A-X-C-T, H-U-J-M, L-I-N-B, D-F-G-V," he read from her paper. "Maybe you should move closer to the board. The drill is A-S-D-F, J-K-L-semicolon. Home row. That's all." He folded the incorrect paper, placed it in his pocket, then rolled a blank sheet into her machine. "Again."

She raised her hands over the keys—so many keys, all a

blur under her fingers! *Hit the A, it's not that difficult. Just put your pinkie on it and press.*

"Again."

The rest of the class clattered away, their eyes fixed on the board. Bells dinged, carriages returned, and everyone else had the hang of it.

"Set your fingers on the keys, as if they were little chairs and you were only resting your hands."

Mollie did. Her right index finger seemed to have a life of its own, though. It wanted most desperately to rest between the N and M.

The teacher stood behind her. He placed his hands on top of hers. His skin was soft and cool and when she looked down, she saw her own fingers below his were still.

"There," he said. "Press the A." He pushed his finger down with hers. "S." Again, a slight pressure. "Excellent . Let's continue." DF. "Thumb to the space bar. Excellent."

The first few days, Mollie went home with a headache from the sound of all the machines, from trying to concentrate for such long stretches of time. Later, the noise did not bother her, but became part of the smugly industrious background of the settlement house itself.

Lunch was taken outside, where children could meet their mothers. The "recreation area," as it was called, was wedged in by the brick walls of factories. Yet in its oddly angled shape, grass had been planted, and the tables were clean as if they'd never once been used. The kids screamed and ran around, sometimes hugging their mothers' knees and eating a bit from a pail brought from home, sometimes smacking sticks against the grass or having pretend sword fights. There was a small tree surrounded by a white picket fence—and oh, how the boys wanted to climb it. They circled around it, hands on their hips, chucking bits of advice to one another on which time of day would be best to sneak past the fence, which times Miss DuPre did not stand watch from her window high above.

Annabelle walked across the grass to join Mollie at a table. "Kids. I swear half of them need a good whack and the other half a bottle of gin."

"You're gonna be a great mother, Annabelle."

"Think so?"

Charlie White straddled the bench across from them. He unknotted the towel that held his lunch: a sausage and a big piece of brown bread, which he immediately ripped into three pieces and shared. He pushed his bowler back on his head and smiled. "Mind if I join you?"

"Looks like you already have," Mollie said.

He slung a hand across the table to Annabelle. "Charlie White. Seen you with the kids, just never introduced myself. What's your friend's name?"

"Lord, you sit right next to Charlie and don't have the manners to introduce yourself? This here's Mollie Flynn."

"Mollie Flynn, Mollie Flynn. Got a good rhythm to it." He held the sausage between his fingers, then finished it in two great bites. The piece of bread he'd kept for himself was swallowed whole. Then he wiped the rag across his mouth and stuffed it in his pocket. "Might be a song somewhere there."

"You a composer?" Mollie asked.

"Composer, clarinetist ... a bit of piano when I feel like it. Pretty good at it, if I do say so myself."

"Then why are you here?"

"Right now? To have lunch with the two prettiest ladies in the crowd. Nothing more a man could want. Well, except to play in an uptown band." He fingered his mustache, as if it was a substantial thing and he was, too. In fact, the mustache was ginger-colored and very fine. Barely worth having at all. "So, what are you doing here?" He said this to Annabelle, his gaze dropping to her stomach.

"I'm a widow." Annabelle tilted her head and frowned.

"Gee, I'm sorry."

"I've been taking in boarders, but the last one drained me of everything."

"You couldn't have seen it coming," Mollie said to her, lowering her voice, as if this was a shameful thing to talk about.

"My jewelry, my wedding ring, even the cat."

Charlie let out a low whistle. "Bad news. Did you tell the police?"

"They ain't good for nothing," Mollie said.

"Did you ever find the fella?"

"She did," Mollie whispered. "This past January. Hadn't seen him in months, then ran into him on Delancey. He was buying a hat."

"With money that was rightly mine," Annabelle added.

"And she was buying a hat."

"And the hatpin got the better of me."

"What do you mean?" Charlie asked.

"Well," Mollie said. She leaned across the table; Charlie followed suit, until their heads were almost touching. "The hatpin launched its way into the fella's right eye."

Charlie drew back and glanced at the girls. His Adam's apple bobbed, and then he forced out a laugh. "You're kidding, right?"

"There's more, though," Mollie said. "You don't mind if I tell, do you, Annabelle, since we've turned new leaves and repented and all?"

Annabelle sighed, and if she'd been wearing her wig; the blonde curls would have bounced ever so sadly.

Mollie pulled at her skirts and kneeled on the bench. "Here he was, a hatpin sticking out of his right eye, and stumbling around. But then he reached in his pocket, and for sure he was going to pull out a gun and shoot us dead—because, see, I was there, too. So, thinking quickly, because I'm a quick thinker, I pull the hatpin from my hair—and it's a long one, very very sharp."

Charlie looked at Mollie, and his eyes narrowed in disbelief.

She saw her hand there, miming the push of the pin. "Well, of course I don't have good aim."

"So I hold him down and she carves a letter in his cheek," Annabelle said. "The letter A, for Annabelle."

"The letter *A* for Assho—" Mollie looked slowly up from Charlie and smiled—"*asking* so desperately for help, didn't I ask you for help, Miss DuPre?"

Charlie twisted around. He lifted his brown derby. "Hello."

"Mrs. Reardon will meet you here directly after lunch, Miss Flynn. To discuss your job."

"Already?"

"It's been a week, Miss Flynn." Emmeline nodded to Charlie and Annabelle. "Mr. White. Miss Lee." She turned and moved to another quarry.

"You know," Charlie whispered, "she's from around here originally. Heard she was a thief once."

"A thief? She wears glasses," Mollie said. "I ain't never known no thief what couldn't see."

"That's what I hear."

"Someone's feeding you a line," Annabelle said. "She's got money written all over her. Listen to the way she talks. You should hear her read books. She's reading *Gulliver's Travels* to us right now and—"

Mollie watched Miss DuPre make a round of the yard, how

she spoke to each person, how she took in everything, analyzing the movements and patterns of the students. Like a thief. Yes. A thief who'd managed somehow to get out. Why in God's name had she come back?

"This whole yard? I'm cleaning this *whole yard*? Look at the trash."

Mrs. Reardon, front-desk matron, said, "The waste bin's in the alley directly right of you. There's a rake, there's a bag, here's a cloth. I'll leave you to it."

Mollie dragged the waste bin from the alley and opened the lid. She surveyed the "recreation and trash area." There were bits of paper and pieces of bread and spills of stew on the tables . "Shit." She pulled a match from her pocket and clamped it between her teeth.

A rap came from a window on the third floor. Mollie looked up.

Emmeline DuPre put her thumb and index finger together and made a motion of pulling a matchstick from her mouth.

Mollie played the match between her lips.

She stared up at the window. She remembered the nuns, then, and thought they might be right: One sin led to another, and the path between was littered with fool's gold. She spit the matchstick to the grass and curtsied.

GOODNESS

THE FIRST THING SHE mastered was the heavy machine that sat in front of her. She had stumbled over the keys, and then memorized the drills scraped in chalk upon the board. This allowed her to look at the enamel letters before her and at least have half a chance of getting it right. For many days, the teacher, Mr. Dunlap, pulled her paper from her carriage, tutted over it, and folded it in his pocket. What he did with all those letters and little words, Mollie did not know. Perhaps he placed them in a file in Emmeline DuPre's office, and the two laughed over her idiocy.

But slowly, and then with a burst of speed, Mollie learned to type. Her fingers, she found, went exactly where she wanted. She did not look at the keyboard, but watched the long metal keys hit the paper precisely and correctly. Mr. Dunlap stopped his habitual turn at her desk and moved on to others. After she was confident in her fingers' placement, she soon grew confident of her speed. She could fill three pages in the time it took others to complete one. She liked the push and *clack*, and the splats of ink, and the *ding* of the carriage return.

Then her fingers found their way without her conscious thought, and she was able to watch the room. Some of her classmates were too tired from working all night to do much more than snore, their heads on their arms, the typewriter a pillow. Working in factories, making candles, turning a cuff, splitting hides, blowing a man in an alley—well, money still had to be made somehow.

And more to the point, she was able to watch where the girls placed their purses and satchels, how the men patted their wallets without thinking, in which drawer Mr. Dunlap chose to store his briefcase. None of them, she knew, had more than a penny or two. And it was not her desire to steal from those who needed those coins.

But she liked to plan how she would steal the coins from the satchels and wallets and Mr. Dunlap's briefcase. A drill and a bit of practice, that was all.

She knew Susie had a picture of her fellow in her satchel, and once she'd finished her drill, she hauled the thing onto her lap and gazed at it like a moron from Barnum's old show. Mollie could walk by, stick both hands and a foot in the satchel, and Susie would still have no idea why she didn't have fare for the El.

Derrick, two seats left, carried a huge wallet in his chest pocket, but that was not where he kept his money. His money was easily heard clinking in the bottom of his lunch pail. Derrick thought this an excellent place to escape the eyes of thieves.

Charlie White had always and only a dime, which he liked to flick up and down in the air at lunch. The dime was to buy dinner for his two sisters and a handful of flowers for his mother.

As for Mr. Dunlap, he may have put his briefcase away in a drawer, but he never locked it up. Mollie could have snuck into the room during any lunch, on the pretense of having left something behind, and taken whatever she wanted. But no doubt there were only folded bits of paper in there, all filled with three- and four-letter words and much gibberish, too.

She took this way of looking into the yard with her, at lunch, and the happy asylum scene became more like the story of the Fourth Ward she lived in. She began to notice that the children played in two separate groups. Certainly both laughed, and their games were much the same. But one side of the yard had heads of red and gold and brown, and names like Ian and Maggie and Ralph. On the other side—just past the tree and far from the alley where the waste bin sat—the heads were dark. The Italians.

And just as the expanse of green grass was divided, so were the tables. For the Italians spoke and shouted in their own language, and the Irish girls and their young men jutted stubborn chins, and spit in the Wops' general direction. Mollie wondered if one of those women might even be her next-door neighbor, but who could know? The Italians all looked the same. Then again, so did the Irish. They were all drab. All rotting like the tenements around them and thinking a flowerpot and a dab of paint would somehow fix everything.

It was when lunch ended that Mollie truly liked her game; it was then she memorized the weft and weave of the settlement-house habits. She loved to rake, particularly in front of the long classroom windows. Through one, she watched the teachers take one last drag of a cigarette before trotting off to teach housekeeping or English, or whatever it was they did. There was a set of deep drawers near the hallway door, and into each, the teachers put their personal items.

Every Wednesday, at precisely 12:35, a huge rump of a man came to visit the teachers and share a few words with some of the students in the yard. He was a Tammany man, most definitely. He stood with his great legs spread wide and confident, a thumb cocked in the pocket of his Fifth Avenue suit. God help the tailor who clothed him in so many yards of satin and silk! "I'm just one of the people," he liked to say. When he laughed, which was often, and often at nothing in particular, his stomach jiggled. His eyes, however, remained steel. After his turn with the teachers in their office and his stroll through the yard, he tilted a head toward the third-story window and gave a quick nod to Miss DuPre. Then into the building he went. The exchange upstairs was meant to be private, but Mollie saw it all from the far edge of the yard. Emmeline's hand held out for a shake, which the man then chose to kiss. Two or three words through empty smiles. An envelope proffered by Miss DuPre and duly pocketed.

The payoff. Of course Miss DuPre would go to the top. No need to pay the cops for protection when you can afford the greed of Tammany Hall itself.

There was a lot of cash floating around somewhere; Mollie guessed it to be in Miss DuPre's rooms, behind the only three locks in the building.

She shook her head. *Now, that*, she thought, *would be an easy take.*

She dug the prongs of the rake deep into the grass. She looked at the lines in the brown soil. What would she do with so much money? Move to Brooklyn, yes, easily and effortlessly. Hire a nanny for Annabelle's baby. Eat chocolate cake and drink whiskey for breakfast. Buy that beautiful hat, with its shades of sunlight, and promenade anywhere she wanted.

She continued to rake, watching bent heads or recitations. The last window let light into the reading class. Emmeline

DuPre taught this class herself. And this was the class where Annabelle sat, front and center, and gazed at Emmeline as if she were the lifeline that would pull her up from the depths.

Mollie expected Annabelle to be turned in her seat, wagging a red-leather boot, passing gossip with the girl behind her. She would have expected her to roll her eyes each time Miss DuPre tapped a stick against the board. But Annabelle did neither of those things. Her eyes were on her book when they were supposed to be, and she recited when everyone else did. All the while, she caressed her stomach.

Annabelle, she realized, was happy. Here, she did not have to think of how she'd feed that child inside her. Here, she did not wonder where the rent came from or if she'd have to haunt the streets again. Here, Tommy did not exist. And here, Mollie thought, Annabelle had finally determined she was good.

No—Mollie would not steal the money from behind the three locks that led to Emmeline DuPre's rooms. To take the money was the same as taking it straight out of the hands of all the people here. To take it from Annabelle.

And to steal from herself the one damn place in the entire Fourth Ward where she finally felt safe.

THE SHELL GAME

BUT THEN DUSK CAME, with real life and all its responsibilities. There was an empty food box at home: This needed filling. There was a second notice on the door regarding rent. There was a trinket box drained of anything worth selling.

Mollie began to haunt the markets late at night, in search of stale bread, half-rotten oysters, and blackened radishes. She dug through trash bins outside saloons, and was often rewarded with entire heads of cabbage and kidney pies not entirely green with mold.

One evening, she climbed the green stairs to the Elevated, looking for a good pocket or two. The path of sin might be lined with fool's gold and guilt, but it also contained the rent.

The platform was heavy with people, all jostling for the best spot, so they might be the one to grab a rare empty seat once the train arrived. Dresses, suits, a pale hand waved above the crowd, a woman's smile in response. There was a boy with blackened face dancing like a minstrel with no music save the squeal of the Elevated's wheels. There was a woman in bright yellow, laughing, a bottle in her hand.

Under a gaslight's frosted globe, Mollie caught a flash of blonde hair, the glint of an eyeglass, a dove-gray cloak. A woman stood separate and apart from the others. Emmeline DuPre waited for the train.

How strange to see her out of her element. How small she looked. She glanced neither left nor right; her face was void of expression. Or rather, Mollie thought, closed and guarded.

Where would Miss DuPre be traveling this time of night? Surely there was a lecture or reading at the settlement house. There was always something or other. Last week, a fat opera singer blared out songs so shrill and sharp, Mollie mistook the great beast in her ruby dress for a cat in full heat. Annabelle pretended to be sick and dragged Mollie from the library. "Even the baby had her hands over her ears," she said. "If that's culture, I'd rather be deaf."

Watches snapped shut. People leaned forward to glare down the tracks. The Elevated was late. In a far corner came a hum and singsong as familiar to Mollie as her own skin.

"Easy as sin. Just watch the shells, watch the shells. Find the penny and I'll give you a dollar."

Three men stood around a small table that could fold quickly out of sight should the need arise. Three shells lay neatly on the wood. Behind it stood a man in a worn gray beaver top hat and red velvet collar, talking smoothly as he lifted each shell. "There. See? Take a close look. Penny's in the left one. Just watch the shell." Around and around went the shells. "There it is center, there it is left, back again, back again, and all in a line. Easy as sin. Drop a three-center and your guess, boys—my game's the cheapest in town."

Two of the men who watched were commuters, not

gamblers. This was obvious in the way one scratched his head under his bowler, the way the other pursed his lips and tried to remember the path of the penny. But the third, timid, narrow of shoulder and hip, a clerk quite gray from spending his day in an office, pulled out a coin.

"You sure you know which one? 'Cause I ain't taking money that should be going to your wife and little ones." The gamesman winked and readjusted his top hat. "And certainly not from some pretty thing you've got on the side."

"I know which one, all right. It's in the left one. Sure as I'm living."

"My friend, the only thing a person can be sure of is being dead."

"It's in the left."

"Coin on the table, then, and let's see if fortune smiles on thee." Slowly, he tipped back the shell. He slid the penny out and tossed it in the air. "Seems I'm slow today. Here's your dollar, I'm an honest man." He pulled a crumpled bill from his pocket. "Now, scram, you're bringing me bad luck."

"Double it down."

"Double it—no, my friend, I said scram."

"Let him do it," the man in the bowler said.

The gamesman rolled his eyes to heaven as if the answer could be plucked from God himself. "Well, being as I'm a charitable man, we'll take one more go. Lay out the bills, my friend, and see if fortune's still kind."

The clerk reached deep in his trouser pocket. He smoothed a bill, matched it with the other, and laid them out. Mollie narrowed her eyes. Two bills, both damp and crumpled. Not a clerk at all. The shill. The one who egged on any sap who approached, to play and win and promise others by example that riches could be had by all.

The game was ignored by the majority, who only wanted

their train and home and dinner. But then, then! A sway of a skirt and a step toward the table. Miss DuPre's gaze flicked over the players, then stopped on the shells themselves. Her foot moved forward, inadvertently, separately from any conscious wish she might have to keep it firmly in place. Her cheeks had a high flush; she raked her lower lip against her teeth.

Mollie thought, *There's the street she came from.* And the fine cut of the cloak, the soft high lace at her throat, the beads in her ears were no more than a costume, a mask, a disguise. The real Emmeline DuPre would open her purse and wager on the shells.

Would she? Would she let go and drop a three-center on the rickety table?

Miss DuPre rolled her hands into tight balls. She tore her gaze from the table and stared at the steel lattice platform beneath her feet. Her face was not blank or guarded or closed now. It roiled and struggled and weighed consequences to actions.

Mollie thought of Annabelle and of the faith she placed in this woman. Good she could not see her now, small and alone, tempted by a crooked set of shells. Crooked herself, mending her ways like any of those who traversed the steps of the settlement house. All that show of power and composure a trick of light.

Emmeline's struggle turned her pale skin even paler. White as the walls of her office. Here was a woman of money and means who could not lose the past. Who had a chance to be rid of the Lower East Side forever, but came back. For what?

Mollie felt a small jolt. She realized she would be disappointed in Miss DuPre if she succumbed to the game.

Please don't, Mollie thought.

Emmeline DuPre jerked and turned toward Mollie. She

blinked slowly, as if trying to put a name to the face she saw before her.

The metal trembled, then shook steadily as the train approached.

She drew herself up, and found her composure. Her expression closed upon itself. If she recognized Mollie, she gave no evidence. She turned to the crowd and lost herself within it.

"Would you have bet, had the train been a minute more late?" Mollie asked under her breath. "Would you?"

April 1883

THE DIME MUSEUM

"… REFUSED TO GIVE ME an ounce of food, they did. Goddamn 'house of God.' A Catholic house of God, mind you." Annabelle pulled the handle of the Love Meter. The metal ball jiggled and remained at STONE COLD. "That's what a baby does to you, Moll. You get to spend your life carrying twenty pounds of fat around for too many months to count."

Mollie dropped a penny in the machine. She yanked the handle and watched the ball bounce and land in a bucket marked ROMANTICALLY INSANE. "I always get that. I think this damn arcade oughtta buy new machines every decade or so."

"And the woman's sitting there with a big green sprig of grass between her teeth. She said, 'A fallen woman is not welcome in the House of God.' And I said, 'Well, what about that girlfriend of Jesus'? What about that virgin birth that don't seem quite innocent to me? You'd turn them away, too?'

Called my child an abomination. And I said back to her, 'You are the abomination. A-B-O-M-A-N-A-Y-S-H-E-N.'"

"I don't think that's how it's spelled."

"But I was so shocked I'd spelled it, I couldn't do anything but stare at her like a drunk. Should have spit on the woman, I should have, calling me names like that. And I should have told her that her husband had a pickle smaller than my pinkie, and doing him was a huge act of charity. But no—I just stood there wondering who in the hell was shouting and spelling 'abomination.'

"The priest is standing right behind her, letting her turn me away. Letting me humiliate myself in the first place for having to stand in a food line. But he steps away, he follows me. Gives me a handful of pennies. Tells me to find God and that there's a basket set up all night to take in babies. 'For those too desperate to keep them.' And you wonder why you and me skip church on Sundays ..."

"Thank God the settlement house don't jam that crap down our throats. Makes me want to turn Protestant."

They wandered the dime museum, stopping a bit at the display of the two-headed calf (stuffed; bought cheap from Barnum's after the Great Fire), and the octopus in a jar. They waited in line at the stereoscope. Above them, a sign read: THE GLORIOUS BRIDGE, EIGHTH WONDER OF THE WORLD. For a penny, a round cylinder whirred before the glass lens, revealing in successive photographs the progress of the new Brooklyn Bridge. Annabelle climbed the steps and leaned into the viewfinder. "It's like I'm watching it be built before my very eyes."

"Let me see." Mollie stepped onto the red-carpet platform and pushed Annabelle aside. How quickly the pictures changed; it made her slightly dizzy. Whoever took the photos had set his camera up at one spot, day after day, year after year. On the horizon, Brooklyn sat like a black hulk. The great expanse of river and its incessant water traffic—sloops and barges and ferries—moved back and forth. Then, block by huge stone block, the towers formed, one per shore, until the grand sharp arches soared and pierced the sky. "Here comes the cable," Mollie said.

"Give me a peek." Annabelle squeezed next to Mollie. They shared the viewfinder, both getting a blurry look at the suspension cables, spun like so many spider's webs.

"Just behind us," Mollie whispered.

They watched the New York bridge platform growing forward, evermore forward, so close to meeting the workers building the Brooklyn platform. So close to that moment New York and Brooklyn would dare call themselves friends. The machine shuddered, and the lens went black.

"The bridge," Annabelle said, with a flounce and a wink at the gentleman waiting in line, "the bridge is going to break in two the first time it's crossed."

"No, it ain't. That's the grandest thing ever been built. That's what we're walking across come May." Mollie stepped off the platform and rubbed her eyes.

Annabelle held out her hand to Mollie. "Give me another penny."

"You got the pennies."

"One more time?"

"All right."

The gentleman, who had been listening along, shifted his umbrella and bowed. "It's a marvelous thing, that bridge, and I certainly understand why one would want to watch again. So, if you don't mind ..." He dropped a penny in the machine. It was apparent, by his gaze, that he liked the way Annabelle's breasts lifted from her dress.

Mollie blinked a few times to get her vision straight. *It couldn't be. Not here.* Yet ... how slim the gentleman was, how his eyes glinted and how he gave her a dancehall wink. How smooth his cheek, how rosy the skin. It was. It was Annie Hindle, male impersonator extraordinaire. This was it, Mollie thought. This was the mark she had dreamed about—a celebrity fast on the town with a load of cash. She could feel it, then, for the first time in months: little stings in the tips of her fingers, the way the racket of the dime museum flattened out to one low sound.

She leaned over the barrier that guarded the whirring machine. "How's it do that? I mean, how's it spinning?" She leaned farther over, trying to locate the mechanism that joined penny to machinery.

"It's a spring," Annie Hindle said in a voice that purred low. "The penny releases the spring, which spins the carousel. And you see the pictures."

"Ya don't say."

The show ended. Annabelle turned from the platform. She gave a woeful look, as if the step down was just too high for a girl to maneuver. She caught the eye of the gentleman (and oh, how embarrassed she'd be later when Mollie told her the truth!), and her cheeks pinked demurely. Annie Hindle lifted a hand to her. Palm up, delicately, as if she'd done it a thousand times before.

Mollie scanned the actress's well-cut coat and trousers. She lifted her right eyebrow, which told Annabelle, *Money's in the left pants pocket.*

Annabelle took Annie Hindle's left hand in hers. "You're so kind." She fluttered her lashes. She gripped tight. The hem of her dress caught briefly under her heel, and she laughed and pulled the fabric.

Perfect. Mollie pushed gently against the roll of money in the clean black trousers. She made an accordion of the pocket lining until the money had no place to go but up and out. She turned back to the stereoscope, as if she'd never moved, too awe-inspired by the concept of a spring.

Annabelle, safely again on the dime-museum floor, tipped her head in decorous thanks. "My husband is—" She pointed vaguely in the direction of nowhere.

"Ah. I see." Annie Hindle lifted her hat. "It was a pleasure."

Mollie slid quietly away. Yes, it was a pleasure indeed.

They waited for the "gentleman" to bend to the stereoscope. Annabelle put her arm through Mollie's, and they strolled to the street.

There would be enough money now, and no more rent notices on their door. They'd waited a long time for that kind of mark. Simple and quick and no need for a knife. How perfect. The arrogant smile and outrageous disguise made it easy to take money from those smooth wool trousers. Annie Hindle would not miss it in the least. Annie Hindle might even make a skit out of it, how she'd been duped by a couple of Bowery Girls. Maybe throw in a bit of a song-and-dance about Annabelle Lee and hint at her luscious breasts. Mollie laughed then, at the thought of it.

"What are you laughing like a fool for?"

"Sure was a handsome gent, wasn't he?" Mollie asked.

"Mmm. What eyes. Did you see those eyes? I'd half a mind to kiss him right there, being he was so kind about helping me down. I wouldn't charge him a cent."

"You might once you saw what he's missing down below."

"Nothing can be missing on him."

"Her."

"What?"

"That there was Annie Hindle. From over at Tony Pastor's. Jesus, Annabelle, you're getting soft."

Annabelle's cheeks reddened to the color of her dress.

"Well, I'll be damned. Just for that he—she—deserved his, I mean her, money taken. Oh, never mind. Let's go get us some oysters and beer."

"You ever wonder," Mollie asked, "why Miss DuPre came back here?"

"She's got a good heart, that's what I know."

"If I had everything in the world, I sure wouldn't share it. Charlie says she was a thief. That means she either hit a jackpot on a mark, or met some fella low-lifing and tricked him into marrying her. How else do you get from here to there?"

"Hard work."

"If you're a man. I ain't never seen you or me or her ever owning some business or factory." Mollie shook her head. "I just want to know, is all."

"What?"

"Why she thinks what she does helps."

"I used to ask you to read menus and sign my name for me," Annabelle said. "You see me asking you for that anymore?"

"No."

"She's got a good heart, and what she does helps me."

"I'm just saying."

"What are you saying, Moll?"

"I'm saying, I'm saying ... I don't know what I'm saying."

"No, you don't. She got friends who don't do nothing but buy hats and travel to Europe and kick their maids. And she couldn't do it. Her guardian told her to make something of herself, something ... what did she say ... 'make something better than some sow-eared fat-hipped silver-spooned lady.'"

"Where'd you hear all that?"

"She told us in reading class."

"In reading class. And all we do is type 'Dad had a lad.'"

"How come you don't like her?" Annabelle asked.

“Don’t like charity workers. You know that. Parade around like they’re on a plane higher than you. And she ain’t really no better than you or me.” She thought of Emmeline in the Elevated, tempted by a set of shells. “She ain’t. Just wants us to believe it.”

“She has a good heart, Moll. Leave it alone.”

They crossed under the tracks of the El, taking to the sidewalk that would lead to Fulton’s Fish Market.

“Sure is a handsome fellow, isn’t he?” Mollie said.

“Who?”“

Annie Hindle. Miss Annie Hindle.”

“All right already.”

“I hate to say it, but that kinda thing sure as hell beats typewriting. The look on your face alone ...”

“Mollie, if you don’t shut up, I’m gonna take that money you stole straight to the first cop.”

HENRY WADSWORTH LONGFELLOW

"I AIN'T NEVER WORN STAYS this tight before." Mollie pulled at her waist, but the fabric was so smooth and taut her fingers found no hold at all. She was left to twist around and blow out all her breath for a bit of relief. She gazed at herself in the long window of the settlement house. She did not recognize in the least the figure she saw before her, though her cheeks pinked with pleasure at how good the figure looked. She had chosen a dress of muted teal that dipped to a V near the waist. The bustle was small, Annabelle having made some alterations, and the material draped in simple, straight lines. The buttons were a darker blue, like the East River on a rich spring day. They began as small pearls near her neck, gradually gaining heft and sheen as they descended down her chest. Over the dress she wore a short jacket with a puff of fabric at the shoulders, tapering to clean lines at her wrists.

Two fine and deep pockets were hidden at each hip. Mollie placed her hands in each, and twirled before the glass.

She had brushed her hair until it shined. It was parted neatly in the middle, small curls at her ears, a tidy bun at the back. She had even touched a pinkie's worth of Annabelle's paint to her lips.

Yes, she was quite pleased with what she saw. "I would say," she said to Annabelle, now clad in a dark gray dress and cloak, both of which shimmered in the morning light yet kept her figure hidden in shadows, "I would say I am almost pretty. Pure Bowery Girl."

"Glad we didn't buy that hat; your head would be too big for it. Haven't I always said ya got natural beauty, Mollie?"

"Well, I don't know about that, but did ya see the greengrocer nod at me? I been used to him glaring at me for years, just because once or twice I borrowed an apple. It's like I got some grand disguise. Kinda like Annie Hindle. I bet a cop would help me across Broadway. I bet you and me could go to the opera and the gents would swoon."

Mollie signed her name with a flourish. She winked at the matron and said, "Didn't recognize me, did ya?"

"*O*, capital *L, Life and*, capital *L, Love*, exclamation point. Capital *O happy throng*, enter, capital *O, Of thoughts*, comma, *whose only speech is song*, exclamation point."

Why, today of all days, did Miss DuPre choose to provide a dictation lesson? Mollie felt split in two—one half in her seat, the other lounging in the sun outside the window. Besides, it was Friday, the day Mollie found most interesting when cleaning up the yard.

"Capital *O heart of man*, exclamation point, lowercase *c, canst thou not be*, enter, capital *B, Blithe as the air is*, comma, *and as free*, question mark."

Miss DuPre's voice rang through the room. She moved between the rows of desks, one hand holding her skirts, the other fingering the three keys tied to her wrist.

It was Friday. The day people came to find Emmeline DuPre and inquire about money possibly owed or promised.

Mollie knew none had any hold on the Do-Gooder; all were from her old life, and had the rags and shiny elbows to prove it. But they came, nonetheless, sitting first in the vestibule, and when turned away by the matron, snuck into the yard and onto a bench for a rest before shaking a fist at the third-floor window.

Even Jip had shambled his way down from the Ragpickers' Lot—and when asked his connection to the settlement house, proudly gave the name "Mollie Flynn." Such went the chatter of the ward, for Mollie had told no one she came here, yet someone somewhere knew.

Click clack clatter ding. Charlie's face was red. He leaned over to read off Mollie's paper. "She talks too fast."

"It's Longfellow, for Jesus and Mary's sake. Don't ya know it already?"

"Can't say it's familiar ..."

"It's boring."

"*What* is boring, Miss Flynn?"

The clack and clatter stopped. Fingers floated in the air above keyboards, curious eyes turned to Mollie. Miss DuPre lightly tapped her keys against her skirt.

"I'm sorry?" Mollie said. "You were talking to me?"

"What is boring?"

"Are we supposed to type that?"

Charlie snorted, then stared at the floor.

"Do you have allergies, Mr. White?"

"Um, no, ma'am, I think I'm coming down with Mr. Dunlap's cold. And I wish him well and hope he comes back soon. But I'm grateful to you for continuing to continue on."

"What is boring, Miss Flynn?" She stared across the classroom, her keys still tapping.

Jesus, this woman let nothing go. Mollie leaned back in her chair and crossed her arms. She felt heat rise on her chest and neck and up into her cheeks. She hated to be stared at. All Mollie had done was whisper to Charlie. Mr. Dunlap wouldn't have cared. But perhaps Miss DuPre was getting back at her. One card topping another. Mollie had caught her at her game; now Miss DuPre wanted to make very sure that she was in charge.

"Are you going to answer the question, so we can complete the lesson and move on?"

"Well, see, it's like this: It's a simple poem with simple short words, and we're already pretty good in here about capitals and exclamation points and such. If you're gonna do Longfellow, why not something more challenging? I mean, it's hot in here. We're gonna all be asleep if we have to keep typing that out. *O Life and Love! O happy throng*. Enter. Blah blah blah."

"I see. 'A Day of Sunshine' bores you. Perhaps you can share a better one? From your vast store of poetry."

"If you don't mind." Mollie stood. "And maybe you can take my seat and I can stand up there."

The floor creaked under Emmeline's foot. Now all eyes were upon her.

"I wager you know how to type, Miss DuPre." Mollie smiled.

They passed each other in the narrow space between the seats; Miss DuPre's skirts were a deep blue, in a tone quite similar to Mollie's. Miss DuPre smoothed the hair at the side of her head; Mollie's own hand raised to do the same. The Do-Gooder settled in Mollie's seat.

Everyone watched her. All fingers were ready and waiting, even Miss DuPre's.

"Proceed, Miss Flynn ..."

"Ahem ...

"It's down in Bottle Alley
Lives Timothy McNally
A wealthy politician
And a gentleman at that.
The joy of all the ladies
And the gossoons and the babies—"

"This is dancehall gibberish." A woman in the front row—who had once called Mollie "Irish trash"—pursed her lips and crossed her arms.

"I'm sorry. I could recite 'Why Did They Dig Ma's Grave So Deep.' I know that one. But let's not, as it's too sad, and crying before lunch just does a number on the stomach. I'll just jump to the chorus."

The woman twisted in her seat. "I said this was ridiculous. She doesn't know any poems. She's just a piece of Irish—"

"At the door on summer evenings
Sat the little Hiawatha;
Heard the whispering of the pine-trees,
Heard the lapping of the waters,
Sounds of music, words of wonder;
'Minne-wawa!' said the pine-trees,
'Mudway-aushka!' said the water.

"Saw the fire-fly, Wah-wah-taysee—

"You're gonna have ta figure out the punctuation on your own,' cause I ain't never seen this written down. Just used to be something us kids liked to shout on the streets. *Saw the fire-fly, Wah-wah-taysee—*"

"*Wah wah what see*? How am I supposed to type Minnie whatever? I'm going home."

"Put your purse down, Daisy Roth, and don't interrupt me."

"But—"

"Maybe next week you can bring a poem for dictation."

"But this is nonsense."

"*Wah-wah-taysee,*" Miss DuPre said. "Capital *W, Wah,* dash, *wah,* dash, *t-a-y-s-e-e*, comma, enter." She smiled at Mollie. "Continue, Miss Flynn."

A NIGHT OF STARS

THE YARD WAS QUIET, save for the *sssh* of cigarette paper being burned. Mollie continued to rake. She did not know what to make of the woman who reclined against the edge of a picnic table and smoked a cigarette in a yellowed ivory holder. The woman stroked three feather boas, pink and dusk and graying white. Her dress was not a dress at all, but a silvery nightgown. Her feet, clad in thin brown boots, were crossed at the ankle, tucked under the bench, as if the boots embarrassed her. *Sssh* went the cigarette paper. The woman blew smoke rings, which she watched until they curled and dissipated in the air. She wore fingerless lace gloves; her nails were ringed in black.

"I can tell you this," Mollie said. "If she ain't come out to greet you, she ain't coming at all."

"I have the patience of a saint." The woman patted the bench beside her. Her words lilted with an accent Mollie could not place: part German, part music. "Come sit by me."

"I got work to do."

"Come sit by me and I'll tell you a story." The woman's eyes, lined in dark kohl that showed her age more than hid it, glittered silver. "Come, come. Even charity workers need a break."

"I ain't a charity worker; I'm just learning how to type."

"An admirable profession. Marking down words. All those words, all that paper. Where does it go, once read and most likely forgotten? Of course, some words are never forgotten. Shakespeare comes to mind, though I confuse the plays. Hamlet and Ariel and Lear could all be in the same play in my little head. It tends toward confusion anyway." Her laugh turned into a small cough. "Come and sit. And you can tell your friends you sat by a duchess."

"A duchess."

"Set your rake down and sit."

"All right." Mollie laid the rake over the trash, to keep it from blowing away. When she sat down, the woman reached out a hand and touched the curl of hair next to Mollie's neck.

"I wore my hair like this as a girl. How old are you?"

"Sixteen."

"Ah, sixteen. The age for love and grand ideals. I was trapped in my father's castle then. It overlooked the North Sea, where the wind shook and rumbled all the days and nights. I loved the wind. I had a long window of cobalt blue glass that I left open summer and winter. You see, I was in love with the gardener on the estate. I'd watch him from my window, watch how gentle those hands were as they snipped the dead buds off bushes. My God, his heart was bigger than this yard. He took to climbing the wall. He had very strong hands. He would wait until the moon shone on the gray stone, then lift himself up and over the balcony. He was a distraction, for my life was only my room and the hollow halls. And then one day, the Russian Ballet came to the city, and off we went in our carriages. And I fell in love again. So I ran away."

"What about the gardener?"

"He was nothing compared to the dance." The woman sighed. "But my mother found me. And promptly tied me to the bed with silken ropes. Prisoner in my own house. The windows remained open, but the gardener did not come anymore. I suppose my mother had found out about that, too."

A movement came from the window of the reading class. Annabelle waved, then gestured that she would meet Mollie outside.

"I chewed through the ropes. I stood on the balcony and jumped."

"You *what*?"

"And I flew. Over the lights of Szczecin, which warmed me enough all the way to Moscow."

"You flew." Jip was a perfectly normal human being compared to this one.

"I danced with the Russian Ballet. Under an assumed name, which I've shortened to Miss Z., as no one in America has the tongue or intelligence to pronounce it. The ballet was a dream. One dream can change your world forever."

"Can you fly now?"

"Too fat."

"Too fat. I see. And how do you know Miss DuPre?"

"I taught her to be a lady."

"Was she really a thief?"

"A thief? My goodness. Did she tell you that?"

"Well, there's rumors going around, and she don't say much except she 'wants to do something meaningful.' It's like she don't really got no past."

"Pasts are better imagined than remembered." Miss Z.

pulled a bit of tobacco from between her front teeth and flicked it to the grass.

"Are all of Miss DuPre's old friends like you?"

"How's that?"

"Nuts."

The door to the yard creaked open. Miss DuPre stood in the frame. "Madame Zwierchoniewska. Come."

It was the first time Emmeline DuPre had invited someone in.

Annabelle cut in front of Mollie and walked backwards. She looked like a cat with a canary. "Mollie Flynn's got a suitor."

"No, I don't."

Annabelle lifted an eyebrow. "Mollie, you need to *look*. You have no idea what's in front of your face."

"I look. I see," Mollie said. "What?"

"Charlie White's coming over. For dinner."

"Why?"

"He likes ya, Mollie. All afternoon he's saying, 'You should've seen her, looked better than Miss DuPre herself.'"

"But I don't—"

"He's not Seamus. And he's not Tommy. That's what matters. He's part of our new life. And he's bringing meat."

And then there was Charlie White, sitting in the one chair they owned, his hat balanced atop a brown paper sack, his clarinet case on the floor. He sat quite stiffly, as if he were at church and fearful of being smacked for slouching in the house of God.

Mollie stood near the door and found herself not knowing what to do. "Can I take your hat?" Mollie asked.

"It's all right."

Mollie noticed the brim had been stitched in places with brown thread.

Charlie blinked, his long lashes touching his cheeks. "I brought some meat. From the butcher shop. Had some extra cuts. I thought we might eat."

"Oh."

They were quiet. Charlie turned his hat round and round in his lap. Mollie wondered if she could actually rip off her thumb, as hard as she pulled.

"You were swell today. Looked just like the teacher. And more fun. *Wah-wah-taysee* . . "

"Miss DuPre was mad."

"No, she wasn't. You're the teacher's pet."

"No, I'm not."

"She sees something in you. I do, too." Then he abruptly got up, and in one stride, stood before the wall that separated the apartment from the Italians. His eyes pored over the newsprint. "This is good. You see this story? It's a serial about a boy who got shanghaied and sent to China. I been reading this story for months. This week, he met a Mongolian king who's got bells hanging from his ears and eyebrows so everyone knows he's coming and can bow accordingly. You been reading this story, too?"

"No. Just that part I pasted on the wall."

"Well, that's lucky. You got the best part hanging right up there. I've half a mind to read it again. I can fill you in on the rest. You'll be hooked, I swear. I'm not saying you have to, I'm just saying it's a good adventure. I'd like to go to sea someday. Not shanghaied of course, just to see things." Charlie's face was red as a tomato. Sweat glistened on his upper lip and he looked like it took great strength to breathe. He sat back down in the chair and stared at his shoes.

The lock in the door tumbled and clicked. And on cue, just like Mollie'd seen in the sketches at the Thalia, Annabelle swooped in. Like the character in a play who'd been listening at the peephole. She set a growler of beer on the table and then winked at Charlie. "Welcome to our house of sin."

He ducked his head in response, and then jumped from the chair, offering it to her. Lord, he was too nice to be believed!

Annabelle plumped onto the bed, and leaned back on her elbows. Her eyes went from Charlie to Mollie and back again. "Anything happen while I was gone?"

"No, Annabelle, it didn't."

Charlie dug his hand into a pocket. "I brought a couple of potatoes, too. And I thought, later, since it's warm and all, maybe we could go on the roof and I'll play you a bit on the clarinet. I just learned a great tune. Do you know 'Lila Lily from Leon'?"

"Can't say we do." Mollie shrugged her shoulders.

After the meal—and how fine it had been!—the three stood on the roof of the rookery. Behind them, pigeons cooed in their cages, and scratched for the food the old man from the first floor fed them.

"Now, that, see, is Orion." Charlie pointed to the sky. "You can tell by the brightness of those two stars, see?"

Mollie did not look up; instead, she watched Charlie. How his arms seemed to enfold the sweep of the constellation. How his cheeks reddened when Annabelle brushed against him. He took her hand in his and pointed her finger at the sky. "There."

Annabelle giggled and simpered. "There's too many up there."

"It's just a matter of focus. You see it, Mollie?"

"Yeah. I see it."

"Sailors know the whole sky by heart. That's how they navigate."

"You want to be a sailor?" Annabelle asked.

"Naw. I'm gonna get myself my own music shop. I'm gonna own three: Yonkers, Brooklyn, and here."

"*Yonkers*?" Mollie asked. "You ever been there?"

"No. Just want three shops. Then I won't be stuck in one all week. I can see different sights. And with the bridge almost done, Brooklyn'll be easy to get to."

"Might as well have shops in Buffalo and Philadelphia, too," Mollie said. "Might as well have one in California."

"You making fun of me?"

"What? No. I'm only saying—"

"She ain't ever been above Delancey," Annabelle said, as if that summed everything up.

"Neither have you."

"Still ..."

"You ain't never been above Delancey?" Charlie asked. "Never gone to Central park?"

"I been meaning to. And anyway, you can see the pictures at the dime museum." Mollie felt like a fool. "We're going to Brooklyn. Soon's we get the money. We even got new names picked out: Mary MacGregor and Sarah Brooks. I don't know why Annabelle likes that name 'Sarah'—it's plain as anything."

"But it's my name."

"If you say so."

"Why do you need new names?" Charlie looked puzzled.

"'Cause we're gonna have new lives," Mollie said. "Why else?"

"I don't get it. It's not like that story, where Nick's friend had to change his name because he killed someone. I mean, you didn't kill anyone ... That hatpin story was a joke, right?"

"Yes, Charles," Annabelle said. "We're good working girls. Evil and us don't mix. So why don't you play us that song?"

He unclasped the well-worn case and twisted the clarinet pieces together. He wet the reed and played. The music was full of life. Mollie grabbed Annabelle and twirled her around, until the stars above them spun in circles of white.

THROUGH A GLASS

"I CAN'T WALK SO FAST, Moll." Annabelle dug the heels of her hands into her lower back. "Jesus, Mary, and Joseph."

"Come on, we're late."

"Good. It'll be ten minutes less I have to sit in a chair."

"I'm the one who should have a bad back, carrying all these books of yours. You can't sit, you can't stand ..."

"And I can't walk as fast as you, so slow down."

"I got a test this morning," Mollie said. "Full set of keys, three five-minute timings. I got a bet with Charlie that I'll be ten words a minute faster than—what are you looking like that for? Jesus, you're turning green."

Annabelle stopped. She made a small gesture with her chin for Mollie to look down the sidewalk.

The Boys. Lounging on the steps of a tenement in a neighborhood that wasn't theirs. They hadn't noticed Mollie and Annabelle. Mollie felt she was looking at them behind glass, that they were curiosities to her, just like the two-headed calf and the octopus in a bottle. She watched them fan themselves with their hard bowlers, for the day was beginning to steam. Mugs laughed and wiped his nose. Tommy was telling a story to Seamus and Hugh; he was playing two characters, one who shivered and seemed to cry, the other with a fist and a scowl.

Mollie had not wanted to see them again. She had taken a woman's money at knifepoint; she had paid Tommy off. That was supposed to be that. She and Annabelle had made a point of taking backstreets to the settlement house. They'd stayed as far away as they could from New Bowery and the Growlers. It was only because they were late that they'd taken Roosevelt instead of Chambers.

"Let's go back, Mollie."

"I got a test."

"We don't need to go that way, do we? They haven't seen us; let's just turn around. I swear to God, I'm not in the mood for them."

Mollie scanned across the street. She found a narrow opening between two tenements: It was possible it had access straight through to Chambers. It was also possible it ended at twelve feet of brick. If they turned around, they'd have to take Batavia, and Mollie might miss the test completely. It was an important test. Without passing, you couldn't move into Dictation II.

Seamus pounded his knee and shook his head. But then the pounding slowed, for he had seen Mollie, and even in her new dress, had recognized her. "Mollie ..."

All their heads turned then. They were very drunk.

"Well, hell in a hand basket, if it ain't the girls." Hugh O'Dowd bowed, blocking Annabelle and Mollie's path. "Look, it's the girls."

"Ignore them," Mollie said.

"Don't you want to say hello to old friends?" Tommy stumbled slightly. He stopped then, flicking dirt from his coat, running a hand over his hair. He looked Annabelle over. "Look how fat ya are, Annabelle."

"I'm not talking to you," she said.

Seamus slung his arm over Mollie's shoulders; he weaved back and forth, and shoved them both in the gutter.

"Goddammit, Seamus, look what ya did to my shoes."

"You fucking him, Mollie girl? Letting some pissant fella up your skirts?"

Mugs blew a few kisses, and Hugh joined him.

"What the hell are you talking about?"

"Think I don't still check up on you?" Seamus dug his chin into her cheek, rubbing and scraping back and forth. "I came by so many times."

"Bugger off, Seamus." She shoved the books in his ribs.

"Jesus, Moll, that hurt."

"Come on, Annabelle."

Tommy walked beside them. "Is it mine? Is it mine, you whore?"

"Shut up, Tommy," Mollie said.

Hugh waddled around them; he'd grown even fatter. "Aw, ya shouldn't call her that, Tommy. It ain't nice. Looks like they've moved up in the world, with those la-de-da dresses. I think you calls girls like that 'Ladies of the Night.'"

Tommy collided with an ash bin. "If that's mine, I'm taking it."

"And what would you know what to do with it?" Annabelle spat out.

"Probably the same's you know what to do with it," Seamus said.

Mugs pushed his way between Mollie and Annabelle, and

lay a heavy hand on each of their shoulders. "Let's go get a drink. There's no reason for us all to fight."

"Where you going?" Tommy asked. His eyes, usually so clear and bright and deadly, were puffy and red.

"None of your business." Annabelle's lips were pressed tight.

"They's going to school," Hugh said.

"What for?"

"I swear to God, Mugs, if you don't let go, I'm gonna punch you in the stomach."

"You wouldn't do that to me, Mollie, would you?" He belched.

"You all stink," Annabelle said. "And I'm on the verge of puking anyway."

"Oh, they got airs, these girls do," Hugh said to Tommy.

"You should miss me, Mollie." Seamus slid a look at her.

There was nothing there, nothing behind the dark, metallic glaze. No fear, no guilt, nothing. Mollie shuddered. This was the man she'd let lay with her. This was the man who once had asked her to marry him, who danced with her at Lefty's, whose hands could be gentle.

All the way down Cherry Street the boys went. All the way to the steps of the settlement house.

"Don't let anyone fool you, girls," Tommy said. "Those do-gooders don't give two shits about you. We're your people. We're who you should trust."

Annabelle held her skirts and walked up the steps, as if she did not see them at all.

"Don't go yet, Moll." Seamus grabbed her and slobbered a kiss across her cheek.

"Leave me alone." She pushed him away.

He dug his fingers into her arms. "Don't tell me of what to do."

"She said to leave her alone." Charlie White knocked Seamus's shoulder. He held a small posy of yellow daisies in his other hand.

"Ah. The pissant faggot." Seamus spread his feet and put his fists on his hips.

"Come on, Mollie." Charlie put his hand on her elbow and turned her to the building.

Hugh shoved Charlie to the ground.

The boys started to kick at him. And then a couple of men bounded down the steps, shoving and punching. More joined them from the street, and it was a mess of flying fists and hats crushed under boots.

"What is the meaning of this?" Miss DuPre strode out to the street. "Stop it! Stop!"

Mollie grabbed at Miss DuPre. "You're gonna get hurt." But she could not hang on, and Miss DuPre landed in the pile.

Mollie knew only one thing to do. At the top of her lungs, she yelled, "*Cops!*" There was just enough time, then, to squeeze in between the men, and drag Miss DuPre out.

Miss DuPre reached into her pocket and pulled out a silver whistle. She blew into it repeatedly; the Growlers ran away, and the students who'd chosen to fight tucked in shirts, wiped their bloody noses, and regained their breath.

She said nothing then, just stared imperiously and waited for every last student to enter the building.

The air crackled all morning. The classroom doors were propped open, no doubt because the energy in each space would have blown them from their hinges. The typing class took ten timings, each one worse than the last. Mr. Dunlap cancelled the test.

"You got a shiner, Charlie." Mollie took his paper from him, looked at it, and clucked. "I should've done it for you."

She unrolled her own paper, and walked up to the front to hand them to Mr. Dunlap. There was a hiss from a desk behind her. She turned to the glare of the German bitch. "What'd you say?"

"I said, 'Irish trash.'"

"What are you, a Danish princess?"

There was a cry from the vestibule. "She bit my baby!"

"I didn't bite him, ya daft bitch, I nipped. He bit my hand. Should be on a rope, he should. I got a bad back—I can't be fending off your monster."

"Aw, shit," Mollie said. She ran out of the class and into the vestibule.

Annabelle paced back and forth, sucking at her finger. "I'm the one bleeding. Probably got rabies now. Look, Moll—look at that little screaming monster. Should've been drowned at birth."

"What did you do?"

"Oh, what I *wanted* to do was—"

"Get upstairs." Miss DuPre stood on the second-floor landing. She was still as death. She held her hands in fists at her sides; the knuckles were white.

"Me or her?" Annabelle pointed at the woman, who hushed her baby. Mollie noticed the child had a very big head and very little eyes. Maybe Annabelle was right to call it a monster. "I'm sorry. It won't happen—"

"Now, Miss Lee."

Mollie paced the far edge of the yard, trying to see into Miss DuPre's office. Two figures, yes, and one with a bent head, but that was all she could make out through the lace curtains.

NO SWEARING
NO RUNNING
NO GAMBLING

NO DRINKING
NO KNIVES OR GUNS
NO WHISTLING (new)

Not one rule about biting babies. Good. No reason then to dismiss Annabelle. And it sounded like self-defense, in a way. All right, she did say "bitch"—but it was entirely possible Miss DuPre had not heard that. And you couldn't kick someone out for one small and first offense.

There was a shatter of glass, then, from the third-story window, and a big book hurtling through the still air, its pages fluttering like wings as it twisted and arced and landed in the yard.

"Jesus, why do bad days always get worse?" Mollie raced across the yard and into the hall. People stood in clumps, and she had to shove and jostle to gain the vestibule.

She caught sight of Annabelle at the front door. Her face was wet with tears. "She's a cruel-hearted bitch, she is. *Bitch*, I tell ya." She pushed the heels of her hands into her eyes. "Oh, Moll."

"What did you say to her?" Mollie demanded.

"She threw a book at me," Miss DuPre said.

Mollie looked at the jagged glass left in the frame and the position of Emmeline DuPre's office chair. Could have been a direct hit.

Emmeline's arms were crossed tight. She paced the small space between her chair and the oak cabinets. "*Nothing* changes here. You give people opportunity and they squander it and spit on it. Too stupid to see they're the problem. Stuck on a wheel like rats."

"What did you say to her? Annabelle don't go around throwing things for no reason."

Emmeline stopped. She crossed to the desk, slid open the

top drawer, and pulled from it a cigarette and silver lighter. She lit it and took a long drag; the ember shook slightly. She blew the smoke through her nose. Only then did she look at Mollie. "How much did that dress cost you?"

"Three seventy-five."

"And Miss Lee's?"

"What does it matter?"

"Where'd you get the money?"

"I thought what we did outside here was of no concern to you."

"You wore it here. I suppose that makes it my business."

"And how do you figure that?"

"I figure, Miss Flynn, that you stole the money to get that dress. I figure, Miss Flynn, that you split the stolen money with Miss Lee and she chose to buy a dress. What else did you do? Go to the theater? Gamble a bit at the Rat Pit? Buy a few necklaces and trinkets to make yourself look nice?"

"I paid the rent."

"Ah, rent, of course. Very responsible of you." She smoked the cigarette down until it burned her finger, then crushed it in an ashtray on the desk. "When is Annabelle due?"

"I don't know."

"Well, how many months has she been pregnant, then?"

"I don't know. Seven or eight months."

"You all shoot yourself in the foot. Every time. And then you blame everyone else for your misery. But there's no one to blame, is there? Only yourself."

"You don't know nothing about our life down here."

"I know everything about down here. I came from down here." The corner of her lip tightened with distaste, with pity, with an edge of anger. "I had my own cellar in The Pits, with my own bed and two dresses and three pairs of shoes. You've heard of The Pits, haven't you?"

The place you went when there was nowhere else to go. A step above hell. The portal to it. The city had tried to close those cellars that honeycombed under the old buildings. They said a grave was kinder to a person than the cellars ever could be. Rat dung and piss, fermenting cabbage from the greengrocers above, rutting sounds both animal and human, walls that seeped water. Yes, Mollie had heard of The Pits. For she and Annabelle had lived there once, too. "And I was a very good thief."

"I don't believe you."

"I had no friends, because I couldn't trust them to be there the next day. I had a father; he used to come round and ask me for money for the church's poor box. He used it to drink. I hated everyone and everything. I hated the men who ran the factories, I hated the workers who couldn't speak for themselves, I hated that my choices in life consisted of being a wife or a whore. I hated it all, and the one way I knew to get back at the world was to steal from the world."

Mollie could barely breathe. She was pinned to this spot, as Emmeline DuPre spoke Mollie's own thoughts.

"And one day, I was too cocky. I'd watched a big boss from a silver-plating factory amble down the steps from his office, and I thought him so stupid and full of himself, so fat with duck and wine, he wouldn't even see me. My hand was in his coat pocket; I could feel the warmth of the wallet. And then he caught me."

"What'd he do with you?"

"I was twelve years old. Too old for an orphanage and too young for jail. That was his thinking, at least."

"So?"

"He took me home. I became his ward."

"You telling me some rich boss took you in? That only happens in books. It ain't a very good story. It ain't believable."

"But it's true."

"Guess you felt sorry for the rest of us. Guess that's why you came back."

"Yes."

Mollie reached in her pocket and found a matchstick. "Since the rules are being broken." She stuck it between her teeth. "So you ain't really any different from the nuns and other do-gooders after all. Filling people's heads with stupid ideas that they might—just might—get their ass out of a crap heap and join the swells up on Washington Square. They'll join them all right. They'll live in their attics and warm their tea and clean their slop buckets. Or work for them—what did you say a typewriter makes? Three dollars a week? Annabelle and me made more than that in a night sometimes. I bet you made a bit on the gaming table yourself. I saw you envying the shells. Bad odds, those shells. And if you were from down here, you'd know that."

"You can think whatever you like."

"I'll tell you what I think. I don't think you came down here until the day you tore down the bathhouse. Made up that story about being a thief, thinking you can get in with all of us. That we're dumb enough not to see through the crap. What do you get out of it all?"

"I get a better world."

Mollie glared at this woman, who was given everything, who came down here to give out scraps. This woman with her beautiful dresses, and rules, and power. "What did you say to Annabelle?"

Emmeline sighed heavily. She neatened her light hair, repinning it, missing a few wisps. After straightening her collar, she sat in the chair behind the desk, the shards of remaining window glass like an angry halo. "I told her I knew of a family that would take the child. In Buffalo."

"You what?"

"I've talked to them—"

"You already talked to them?"

"They have money. They have things—"

"You *talked to them*? She loves that baby. Jesus, she loves that baby more than anything in the world. Why do ya think she came here? For her own amusement? You think she can't be a good mother?"

"I think she has no idea how hard it's going to be. I don't think *you* know how hard it's going to be."

"As if *you* know. I don't see none of your kids running around."

"I've seen what happens."

"She trusted you to help her."

"I am," Emmeline said.

"By taking away the one thing she loves? By saying she ain't as good as some rich family in Buffalo?"

"I am giving the baby—and Annabelle—a chance. My God, there's no father. Neither of you have any idea—"

"She trusted you."

"She still can."

"No—you're just like the rest of them. Playing God. Deciding who's worth it and who's not. Annabelle Lee saved my life when I didn't want to save it myself. She fed me, bathed me, and gave me a name, and I will never, ever forget that. And anyone that hurts her hurts me, you get it? No rich family in Buffalo will ever give that baby half the love Annabelle's got to give."

"Don't throw everything away because of her."

"Go to hell, Miss Emmeline DuPre. And I hope that gets me dismissed, 'cause I ain't never coming back, either. Wish I'd been the one to throw that book, 'cause I swear to God it would have hit."

"My name was Caroline O'Leary. I came from the same streets you did. I never forgot them. Because these streets can be *better* if one person does one thing to change them. Think of what would happen then. Think of the difference."

"It ain't gonna happen."

"One thing. That's all."

"Like taking Annabelle's baby."

"No. Like showing you there's more to this world than stealing. Don't you see that? I am trying to help."

"I don't want your help. I don't need your help. And Annabelle don't need the kind of help you want to give, so like I said before, go to hell."

May 1883
THE RAT PIT

JIM CROWLEY'S RAT PIT looked as good as its name. It was a squat and squalid yellow building, smashed between two tenements like a rotten tooth. The windows were hidden behind padlocked black shutters. The doorway was rimmed with yellow globes that spilled jaundiced light across the faces of all who entered.

The boys and men came in droves; the Rat Pit on a Sunday was the best game in town. They sat, leaned, and yelled from circles of benches that seemed to hang above the pit itself. Two small gates faced each other from across the dirt playing field. At a signal, the gates were lifted open and the bout began. Six rats against one very vicious little terrier. A bet could be made for the rats to overtake the terrier, or vice versa.

Mollie sat squeezed between Seamus and Mugs on the highest rung of benches. Hugh sat directly in front of them; Tommy lounged to Mugs's left. He didn't watch much of the game. His attention was directed to Annabelle; his eyes claimed her as his, his arm encircled and kept her. Annabelle was the plaything of a king.

It had been easy to go back to their old ways. Mollie laughed at herself for even calling them that, for had she ever left those ways thoroughly behind her? No—only in the hours between seven thirty and five o'clock. She did not miss the daily settlement-house pattern, the rotten monotony of it—no—for it could never compare to the brittle crack of this life, to the lights around the Rat Pit entrance and the dusty green curtains of Lefty Malone's.

And Lord, how nice it was to stay up all hours, to drink too much beer, to sleep in forever. To not follow rules!

Wasn't it nice? Wasn't it?

There was still the tugging doubt, the one she squeezed into a little black ball and shoved below the drink or the music or the game. The small doubt, which tiptoed across the floor of their room in the small, quiet hours of morning, kept Mollie awake. She knew when it would appear, for it came fast on the heels of a dream that constantly repeated itself. A dream of a huge spinning wheel that bore down on her no matter how fast she ran.

It was not a regular wheel: Between the spokes, she saw Jip from the Ragpickers' Lot dancing a jig, his left arm flinging about of its own accord. There was Seamus bringing her a bouquet of tight red curls, Tommy slicing the hand of a sailor, Charlie swimming in a sea of stars. Annabelle was little again, as she was when she'd first found Mollie—she sat in Emmeline DuPre's lap, listening to a bedtime story and playing with a curl of her own wig. Mollie called to her and called to her, warning her that the wheel would roll and Miss DuPre was about to throw her out. But as the wheel turned, no one fell. The faces blurred into white noise, and it was then that Mollie knew it was headed toward her.

She often wondered what the dream meant, but she did not wonder about the doubt that followed. Its voice had started in the harsh murmurs of the Do-Gooder and ended in her own. It asked her to look—really look—at the newspaper glued to the walls of a windowless room, at the faces of those whose money and cuff links she stole, at Annabelle who complained of thick ankles but did not give a thought to how she would feed the baby once it came.

Mollie Flynn was of a practical nature. She knew the patterns of the Fourth Ward, and when the doubt grew large, she knew the only way to ignore it was to plan her next day. What street to travel, what game to play. A small swoon in the middle of a lunch crowd? A quick grab and run from the grocer's? Doubt stopped her hands; planning kept them still. And goddamn the Do-Gooder, who thought her stupid. *Stuck on a wheel like rats.*

Seamus pulled at the sleeve of her dress, disrupting her thoughts. "Where'd you get this dress?"

"What's it matter to you?"

"Jeez, Moll, I just wanted to say ya look like a queen in it." Seamus frowned. He crossed his arms and stared hard at the ring.

Mugs leaned to her from the other side. "I bet on the next set of rats. Looked particularly mean and hungry to me."

Hugh turned around. "It'll be the terrier this time. Shifty's gonna do them all in."

"Ah, you don't know nothing," Mugs said.

Hugh shook his head. "It'll be your waste of money, my friend."

Mugs patted Mollie's shoulder. "Glad to see you again, Mollie. We was worried, what with you and Annabelle not being around."

"Least ya came to your senses," Hugh said. "When Tommy heard that do-gooder was gonna take the baby, well, we had ta convince him not to burn the whole charity down. Course, Dolores ain't taking it so well, now that Annabelle's back. She ain't been dancing at her best."

"Shut up, Hugh." Seamus smacked the back of his head.

"Tommy was seeing Dolores?" Mollie asked. "The redhead who lost her top that one night?"

"Well, he's a man and all. Can't expect him to—"

"And who were you seeing?"

"No one, Moll. I love you. Jesus, I fixed a guy for you."

The bell clanged.

"All right, all right, here we go." Mugs leaned his bulk forward as the gates were lifted. "There he is, Mollie. Rum Kelly's new dog. Shifty. Ain't he a beaut?"

The terrier did not look much good to win, as he missed an ear and eye and various patches of fur. Rum Kelly leaned over the railing of the pit. He chewed a cigar and cheered his dog with foul and loathsome words.

The rats, who had run right over one another when the gate lifted, moved into a row. Their eyes fairly glittered with hatred. One rat ran across the ring, and bit the terrier's head. The others swarmed Shifty, and the dog was lost under their undulating bodies. Shifty got hold of one rat's tail and flung the creature to the side. But the others bit and lunged, and Shifty fell under them, his shrieks joining those of the spectators. Then he was silent as death, too still to be anything but. Mugs bounced up and down in his seat.

Then, one leg at a time, Shifty gained his footing and shook the rats off. He seemed, this one-eyed terrier, to have suddenly grown three mouths, as one after another, he dispatched his enemies. Oh, how the crowd roared, and Rum Kelly roared louder than them all. He stood up and bowed, all the while saying, "That's my Shifty and ain't a rat in New York gonna best him."

Mugs crumpled his tickets and shook his head. Hugh laughed in glee.

There was a lull as the gatekeepers entered the ring to clear up the carnage. Next would be a dog fight, and the odds were even.

The gatekeepers raked the dead rats under the stands. One of the rats twitched, and his black eye watched the boot descend to his skull and crush it flat. It was nothing to the gatekeeper. Nothing in his face changed as he twisted the boot into the dirt. He'd go home after the fights were done and kiss his wife and hold his children and put those boots up on the stove grate.

Mollie stood up and shoved her way past Mugs's knees. She stepped on Tommy's foot and turned her head so she wouldn't see Annabelle or the bounce of blonde curls in her wig. She'd grown used to the Annabelle at the settlement house, who kept her dark hair simple. Mollie pushed through the people who lined the stairs. Bits of losing tickets fluttered from the floor. She shoved open the door, and gulped for air.

Then there was a warm hand on her back, moving in slow circles. "They didn't need to kill that rat. He had a few good fights left in him."

"What'd we do, Annabelle?"

"I never asked you to leave."

"Look at my hands. They're shaking again. I look at people and *see* them, not even a place in my head for figuring out the game. I get it all planned the night before, but ya know what I do? Walk down and watch them finish the bridge. Look at the water and think—there's Brooklyn, there's where we're going. But you're gonna marry Tommy and what the fuck-all is gonna happen then? Is he what ya want, Annabelle? I mean, look at you—you ain't worn that wig since ya walked the streets."

"He's never seen me without it."

"He don't know who you are, then. *I* know who you are." A tear burned down Mollie's face. She wiped it away. "I know ya want to read. I know you're gonna love that baby. I hated that baby, Annabelle. I can still hate that baby. But I know you love it. And I love you. You and me's family. And I went to that stupid settlement house ta make you happy and ya know what? I was happy, too. 'Cause I thought, *We're gonna go to Brooklyn and I'll get a job—a real job. And we'll have a place with a window and you and the baby can look out and see the sun.* You think Tommy's gonna give you that? Jesus, he took half your wages, Annabelle. What do ya think he's gonna do with—"

Annabelle stepped back. "Don't say that."

"There's people better than him. Look at Charlie. Doesn't even know what a mark is. Don't ya want someone like that? Don't ya?"

"If you were a man, I'd marry you, Mollie Flynn. But you aren't. And Tommy is. And I love him."

"You love him when you wear that wig and pretend to be someone you're not."

"And what are you pretending to be in that dress?"

"I ain't pretending to be—"

"A do-gooder," Annabelle said. "You look just like her."

"You've gotta be kidding me."

"Go back to the settlement house, Moll."

"Not without you."

"I ain't going back there. Telling me she's got some family for my baby. As if it ain't related to me at all. As if it's some book or something you lend out. Aw, hell." Annabelle shook her head. She took in a breath, lifted her shoulders, and then reached into a skirt pocket. "Here. Put your hand out."

Mollie complied. She felt a slip of paper placed there, then a round metal object. "What's this?"

"Look."

It was a watch, a woman's watch to be worn like a necklace, simple and silver-plated, with two straight hands and a mother-of-pearl face. The ribbon was a deep teal, to go with the new dress.

Annabelle put the ribbon over Mollie's neck. "You'd think after all these years, you'd've kept one of those watches that passed through your hands."

"It's beautiful."

"I been looking at it in the pawnshop round the corner from the school forever, wondering, would she..."

But Mollie had stopped listening. She stared at the paper in her hand. A crude little flower was drawn in the bottom corner, and red rouge had been fingered into the petals. The black letters had been worried over, and in some places, the ink had pooled and soaked the page:

Hapy Berthday—from me.

"It's my birthday? I forgot."

"It's tomorrow ya daft—Go watch them finish that bridge tomorrow, then we'll have oysters and beer at home at four thirty." Annabelle swung a red leather shoe. "Naw—make it four thirty-nine. Just so I can make sure you're using the watch." Annabelle put a hand on Mollie's shoulder.

"This is the nicest thing—"

"Aw, don't go soft on me. I hear there's some timing things need to be done to figure out if the brat's really due." Annabelle's stomach was heavy and low, filled with a new life she was soon to throw away. Like the boys who played King of the Mountain in the tenement yard. "I got to go back now.

And you only got two blocks to walk from here to eat your hat and somehow get your ass back in."

"Annabelle—"

Annabelle swallowed. She leaned in and brushed her lips against Mollie's cheek. "I think I did right by you after all."

A BIRTHDAY

3:35 P.M.

The ticket office had already been constructed along the approach to the great bridge, with barricades to separate people into organized lines. Above the fluttering red awning, a sign of white letters against shiny black paint read: OPENING DAY MAY 24TH. 2:00 P.M. 1 ¢ TOLL.

There would, of course, be a similar ticket booth on the other side of the East River, with a similar sign. Twenty thousand people were expected to cross the bridge from New York to Brooklyn, and to tip their hats to the twenty thousand expected to cross from Brooklyn to New York.

Mollie looked beyond the booth to the gray stone of the New York tower. She followed the curved lines of the suspension cables from their huge casings to their highest point at the top of the tower and their downward swing across the river. There was nothing in the world that matched the height of this tower; even the round arches that formed the underpinnings of the roadway dwarfed the buildings around her. The Elevated railway, passing under one such arch, looked like a toy pushed by a bored child, minuscule and inconsequential.

Mollie read from a penny pamphlet she bought at a pushcart already hard up against the entrance to the promenade.

HEIGHT OF TOWERS: 276 ½ FEET

HEIGHT OF TOWER ARCHES: 117 FEET

HEIGHT OF ROADBED ABOVE THE RIVER: 135 FEET

NUMBER OF CABLES HOLDING THE BRIDGE: FOUR

LENGTH OF CABLE WIRE HOLDING THE BRIDGE: 3,600 MILES

Barricades had already been set up on Roosevelt; by the end of the week, Cherry and Water streets would be thus blocked off. Temporary tents of all colors lined the sidewalks—each offering postcards and souvenir rings and bowls and cups, some offering hot corn or smoked fish. Mollie wandered the forming festival. Tickets would officially go on sale at eleven thirty P.M. the night before opening day. But there were sure to be sharpers around, with half-official tickets. With twenty thousand expected to pass this side, well, no one would have the time to thoroughly check the tickets for accuracy. And with twenty thousand people and umbrellas and picnic baskets, who would notice two more passing? Who would deny Annabelle and Mollie their chance to see the world from the height of heaven?

She picked up and examined a postcard showing the Royal Baking Company. Obviously the artist was under contract with the company, for the yellow building—at only six stories!—had been painted bigger than the river itself and appeared a story taller than the bridge.

She caught a movement, then, from the corner of her eye. Just to the right of her, a young girl stood. Hair slightly dull, clothes indifferent and forgettable, no expression on her face, fingers that flicked through pages of a book about the making of the bridge, eyes that did not stop on pictures or words.

Mollie fanned herself with the postcard, then decided to buy it for Annabelle. She thought she would give it to her, writing on it: *Please cross the bridge with me. 2:00 p.m. May 24.* Annabelle would be pleased that Mollie had used her watch. She reached into her pocket for a coin, and did not startle to feel other fingers there.

"I wouldn't do that if I were you," she said.

The girl looked up at her; she was no more than ten. Her brown eyes ricocheted side to side, looking for some exit or excuse as to why her fingers were in Mollie's pocket. She had not been in the game long.

"Listen," Mollie said, "it's my birthday and I don't feel like having my pockets picked. So bugger off to the other side of the street."

The girl swallowed. There was soot on her cheek, and Mollie knew she had probably slept on some grating hard by a building warmed by the sun.

"Can you read?" Mollie asked.

"Bible."

"Ya know where Cherry Street is?"

"What, ya think I'm stupid?"

"There's a building there got new columns and clean windows. If ya want something better, walk up the stairs. And don't mind the matron, she's only bitten a couple of people. And here's a few pennies. Now get out of here."

4:31 P.M.

Mollie circled the yard once more. She wiped her shoes

against the back of her legs and shook out her dress. The watch ticked against her chest. Above her, a confusion of laundry snapped in the breeze, strung from front building to the rookery, all mixed up. Mollie wondered if people ever fought over pieces, tugging back and forth on those that were newest and least gray.

4:32 P.M.

"So, I'll be early." She stepped into the hallway and started up the steps. The higher she climbed, the more the narrow stairs smelled. The warm days brought out the reek of eggs and cabbage and sweat. She slipped on the fourth-floor landing and grabbed at the wall to keep from falling. There was an overturned pail in the corner. The whole of the space smelled sourly sweet. Beer. And brine, thick, heavy, and viscous. The smell of oysters. She lifted her skirts, for the stairs to her floor were wet, too. The stench of the beer and the brine grew, as if the walls of the building had been soaked in a beer vat, then rinsed in the East River.

Her foot landed on something hard and sharp, and in the dim light, she saw the craggy sharp shell of an oyster.

There, at the top of the stairs, a scattering of oysters, a shallow sea of brine. Another pail, on its side against the wall.

Something's wrong, Mollie.

Her own door, open, the kerosene light, brought out only for special occasions, now bright.

It's all right, Mollie, she's just surprising you. You'll turn the corner, and there'll be a big bowl of oysters. And Annabelle will clap and say, "You never remember your birthday, because you're a daft one. See how you need me, Mollie Flynn?"

Mollie stood at the threshold to her room. The walls were festooned in garlands of color: red, pink, robin's-egg blue.

Annabelle had cut her old street dresses into strips and tacked them to the walls in bunting and flowers.

And there was Annabelle herself; she sat on the edge of the bed, a hand gripping the mattress on either side. The front of her dress was wet and dark.

"Look at that," Mollie said with a laugh. "It'll take a century to get that oyster smell out."

"I tripped on the stairs." Annabelle blinked—very slowly—like a fancy doll when you sit it upright. She shifted her foot; it was not clear, salty brine that pooled on the floor, but the deep crimson of blood.

"Oh, my God." Mollie backed away. "Somebody help me," she whispered. "Oh, God, please, somebody help me." She slipped on an oyster—they were like marbles; she could not gain a foothold anywhere. "Help me!" She scrambled for the door next to theirs, and pounded. "Please help me."

The door creaked open, just enough so a child's brown eye looked out at her. She pushed against the wood, saw them all there—saw the scissors and needles frozen in air. "Help me!" Then fabric moved and scissors dropped, and the Italian woman moved to Mollie, shushing her children and waving a hand at the men to stay back.

They were around the corner, then, and the woman crossed to Annabelle. She placed an arm around her and laid her in the bed. She pushed the stained skirts high up Annabelle's waist, then cut her stockings out of the way.

Annabelle's breath was shallow and quick, and with each breath came a spurt of blood from between her legs.

"*Tovaglioli*." A gesture toward the rag in the bucket.

But it wasn't enough, soaked through within seconds.

"Più. Ho bisogno di più."

The woman pointed a finger at the wall. Mollie yanked the fabric down and pushed it to her. Watched her wad it up—red, pink, robin's-egg blue—and press it between Annabelle's thighs. Watched the blood bloom and blossom, turning everything the same shiny scarlet.

"What's happening to me?" Annabelle took in a heaving breath. "Mollie—"

The Italian woman murmured something to Annabelle, who only stared, opening and closing her mouth, trying to catch a breath.

"Chiama un medico."

"What?" Mollie couldn't move. She felt she was underwater, under the briny sea and this woman was a great big fish floating by.

The woman grabbed Mollie's elbow and shook hard. "*Medico, medico*. Doctor!"

Batavia Street. Smoke brick building and a sagging door. Sign in the window. Dr. Aloysius Smith, the *S* in "Smith" barely readable, gold stencil faded spider's-web thin. Mollie shoved open the heavy door. Inside, twenty or more children and mothers. A man with a long mustache holding his cap around his hand.

Toward the back of the room, a tall woman scratched at a pad and called out names. Her face was rigid, her cheeks pocked from some childhood illness. She looked at nothing but her pad of paper.

Mollie stepped over knickered legs and a game of marbles. "I need you to come."

"Name?"

"Not me, it's my friend. She fell on the stairs, she needs a doctor."

"So does everyone in this room."

"But I got money. I got lots of money, please, he has to come."

"Bring her down here."

"She's bleeding. She fell on the stairs. She's pregnant."

"Dr. Smith's out at the wharves. Get some of the women from your building to help. I'd come but I'm the only one here. I'm sorry."

Out the door, then. Where else, where else? She spun in a circle: silver plating, greengrocers, pawnshop. Who could help her?

FREE LECTURE. White sign edged with a fancy black border. Mollie jumped the steps and careened through the door.

"No running—it's on the *rules* list." Mrs. Reardon folded her arms and tutted.

"Where is she?"

"Miss DuPre?"

Mollie slammed her fist into the wood of the high counter. "Goddammit, tell me where she is!"

They ran down the street together. Mollie hiked her dress to her knees for speed. She wanted her old dress, with all that space to move her legs.

"When did you find her?"

"Around four thirty. She fell on the stairs. She was carrying two pails, there's no railing."

"What time is it now?"

Mollie grabbed the watch at her chest. "Five o'clock. Five oh-one."

And then Emmeline DuPre lifted her skirts, too, and didn't apologize to anyone as she shoved her way past.

People in the hallway, watching. Water boiling on the stove, white steam. A lump on the mattress, between Annabelle's feet, black and still, rolled in fabric and quickly moved to the floor. Annabelle's shoes darker red. Skin like ash mixed with snow.

Her breath was hard and rough. One, two, three. Nothing. Palms clenching. Legs splayed. A clutch of breath then.

The Italian woman's forearms were stained; there was a swipe of red on her cheek. She looked up at Emmeline. "*Medico?*""

No." Emmeline touched Mollie's shoulder. "Hold her hand. There's nothing else to do."

"No! Give me more rags. Look, she's still bleeding. Please, Annabelle, ya gotta stop, now, this ain't funny." Mollie scratched at the newspaper on the walls. She ripped at the pieces, and then crushed them together. She crouched on the bed, holding the papers to Annabelle with her knee, leaning over her and pushing at her shoulders. "It's gonna be all right. Annabelle, listen, it's gonna be all right. Don't I always look out for ya? Don't I always?"

"I'm scared, Mollie."

Mollie rubbed Annabelle's cheeks, but they did not pinken. "Oh, Annabelle, it's all right, see? Just breathe right. Take another breath." She squeezed her hands. So limp. Mollie entwined their fingers. "I got tickets to see the bridge, Annabelle. And soon, we'll have a real room, with a window. You can sit and look at the sky and dream. I got it all planned. I love you more than the world." She leaned forward, her cheek against Annabelle's; she felt the bones through her skin. "God, she's not breathing. Please ..."

Annabelle pressed against her, and took a gulp of air. "One oh-six Monroe Street. Tell Elizabeth Brooks her daughter Sarah has died."

"You ain't dying."

"Hold my hand, Mollie."

"I'm holding your hands, can't you feel?"

"I was bad. She always said I was bad. You'll be good, won't you, Mollie?"

Annabelle's fingers gripped Mollie's. Her limbs went rigid, then her body convulsed. It was terrible how she stared, her eyes so black. "The baby?"

Black lump now on the floor. "She's all right, Annabelle. She needs ya."

Annabelle's mouth opened wide, then clamped down. She moaned, then shuddered once, then let go of Mollie's hands. "

Annabelle, oh, please, wake up." Mollie slapped her cheek; she pulled and pushed at her shoulders.

The only sound was the rolling boil of the water on the stove.

Mollie lay down, her head in the crook of Annabelle's arm, her palm holding the little watch against Annabelle's chest. She listened to the tick, steady as a heartbeat.

5:09 P.M.

She placed her fingers on the soft, cold skin of Annabelle's lids and drew them shut.

The boys who hauled the mattress to the yard and now scrubbed the floor with stiff brushes were named Giuseppe and Paolo.

The woman was Sofia, and the red stain on her cheek was permanent, a birthmark. She showed Mollie how to loop the stitch in the muslin, then held the fabric closed as Mollie turned the thread. Before completing the seam, Mollie laid the needle on the table. She placed a penny on each of Annabelle's eyes, to ward off evil spirits and bring her good luck and fortune.

She slept behind the stove in Sofia's front room and shivered all night. There was an old woman on a cot, the grandmother, who either snored or watched her.

In the morning, the men came. Heavy feet on the stairs. A whistled tune that reminded Mollie vaguely of one of the dancehall songs.

Emmeline DuPre kept an arm around Mollie's waist.

Count the nails as they hammer the coffin tight. The pine is new and soft.

"Step back," the one with the black whiskers said. "Give us some room, the stairs is tricky. Don't want to end up in Potter's Field yourself." His laugh cut Mollie in two.

THE WHEEL OF FORTUNE

MORNING. A BARE WIRE bed frame, a worn blonde wig hanging from a post, empty walls. A chair moved aside to let the cheap coffin pass. On the hook behind the door, a long black coat with a breast pocket full of coins.

Mollie put the coat on, buttoning it from knee to neck. She had not changed her dress; there was nothing to change into, anyway. She did not lock the door as she left.

She strode down New Bowery, looking neither left nor right. She did not apologize to those whose shoulders she bumped, and it made no difference to her if they cursed her or shook their fists.

Her hair, coming loose from its pins, was much like the blinders of a horse. She did not push it away from her face. She kept her hands shoved deep in the pockets of her black coat.

It was a fine day, not a day for coats at all. But she felt as if her skin was inside out, raw and vulnerable.

All she could do was keep walking, keep her mind blank, not remember that the room at Oak Street would be empty tonight or that she had two tickets to cross the bridge.

There were meaner streets in the Fourth Ward than Oak Street, with smaller rooms and darker stairs. There were rooms with fewer things in them than hers: wash basin, stove, a mattress of straw upon the floor. A rocking chair black with grease and age.

106 Monroe Street. Tight by Corlears Hook and the snaking bend of the Elevated.

Elizabeth Brooks sat in the chair, her body squeezing and spilling between the slats. Her hair was filthy, matted down, and tied with a piece of string. Mollie saw nothing of Annabelle in her. At first, she thought she'd found the wrong person.

"Are you Elizabeth Brooks?"

"If you're looking to collect on a bill, I don't have anything for you."

Mollie stood in the middle of the room. So this was the woman who had thrown her child to the streets. Who once called herself a mother. Who in all the years Mollie and Annabelle roamed and wandered, had hardly been mentioned.

"Your daughter Sarah is dead."

The woman pushed her tongue against her lips, as if expelling something bitter and unexpected. "I don't have a daughter named Sarah."

"There'll be a wake. At Lefty Malone's tonight. If you once cared for her—"

"I don't have a daughter."

Mollie turned to leave. She had delivered the message.

* * *

She found Hermione Montreal dozing in her doorway, her cards closed between her hands. Mollie rolled the two dollars she'd made by pawning her shoes, replacing them with others that clicked and banged against the cobblestones. She placed the bills under the old lady's bent finger.

Hermione snorted, and glared at Mollie from her blind eye. Her fingers crushed the bills and shoved them between two buttons of her dress. Her lips stretched across her gums. "Indulge an old woman?" She spread the cards on a dirty blanket before her. "Three cards: past, present, and future."

"Nah." Mollie cleared her throat. "Not in the mood."

"You used to come to me with a friend. I gave you whiskey and cookies. Good girls you were." She scraped her nails through her white hair. "Now there's a bridge where my home was. Well, the Wheel of Fortune always turns ... and the only thing to do is jump on. Crush you otherwise, it will. But you know that." She coughed. "Have an extra penny for a pint?"

So the wheel turned, in the same circle that razed old women's homes, sent kids to sleep under rags, provided baskets at churches for women to leave their babies, gave wages that barely paid rent but provided enough for drink, built tenements without water in each hall or rails on the stairs or toilets in the yard. It was the wheel Mollie'd thought she'd been running from. It was the wheel she'd really been a passenger on.

The dusty curtain was drawn across the stage, and the tables and chairs were mostly empty. Nipsy snapped out dance tunes on the rackety piano, as if this were nothing more than an extension of the nightly show. The gaslights along the walls were set low, in some sort of respect. The boys sat at their normal table, right up near the now-hidden stage. Hugh ran his thumb over the top of a deck of cards. Mugs stared into space. Seamus drank: one beer after another, in huge angry gulps.

And Tommy sat with a leg crossed, in a black suit still showing creases from being taken from a box. He did not drink; he did not move. A stone statue, but for a tic at the corner of his left eye.

Mollie sat alone. She had ordered two stale beers. The only drink she could afford. Lefty had closed the dancehall, had a sign painted saying CLOSED FOR DEATH, but he still charged for drinks. She knew the drink was mixed with other things—camphor, benzene, and God knew what—and the first sip burned. She took another sip, looked around the tired room, with its smoke-black ceilings and tattered flags and dried vomit on the floor. The fuck-all life of the Fourth Ward. The dead horse rotting on the corner. The boys still at their table, waiting for this to be over. Not a sign of Miss Emmeline DuPre or Charlie White or any of the girls from the settlement house who knew Annabelle Lee when she was happy.

No one spoke of Annabelle. No one spoke to Mollie.

She drained the first glass, and the second did not sting. It turned her blood to molasses; her cheeks and arms warmed and went numb. She stared at the kerosene lamp on her table, sputtering as it reached its end. The smoke curled from the glass lamp. And she thought, *Annabelle*. Annabelle, with that goddamn wig she wouldn't step outside without. Annabelle, who fluttered her lashes at any man she thought might have the money to pay her. Annabelle, who she'd waited for, stolen and borrowed money for, counted the days for. Annabelle, who'd had a chance to be something better and had thrown it all away.

Why'd she have to carry two pails up those stairs that had no railing? Stupid it was. Stupid, stupid Annabelle. Stupid Mollie for not being there sooner to help her.

She hiccupped. She looked to the boys to see if they had

noticed. No. She stood and the floor swished under her. Holding the back of her chair, she waited for her head to clear enough to find Nipsy. "Play 'Annabel Lee,'" she said.

"Don't know it."

"Ya know everything else."

"How about 'Danny Boy'?"

"Well, she weren't a boy and her name ain't Danny. And I want ya to play 'Annabel Lee.'"

"I don't—"

"Then don't play nothing."

The front doors ratcheted open, and the dust in the room hung in the light. The Growlers flicked their knives open, and squinted into the brightness. Two figures—could be the Rum Runners coming in.

But no. Mollie saw the soft outline of Emmeline DuPre's dress, and as the door shut and her eyes adjusted, found Charlie White's oft-mended hat, being worried in his hands.

"Ya missed the best part of the wake," Mollie said.

Charlie stepped forward and kissed her cheek. "I'm sorry." He glanced then at Seamus. "He's not going to hit me if I sit with you, is he?"

"No one's gonna hit anyone," Seamus said. "You wanna sit with her, then sit with her. Being as you're all too good to sit with us."

Charlie pulled out two chairs, and gestured to both Mollie and Emmeline DuPre.

Emmeline slid into her seat. She looked out of place, as much as she claimed to have once thieved on these streets. She glanced over her shoulder to the long bar, where Lefty Malone stood wiping a glass.

"I'm opening at six," he said. "Gives you fifteen minutes more." He shook his head and blew a breath from under his long mustache. "Not much of a wake."

Emmeline rested a hand on Mollie's arm. "Sit."

Mollie unbuttoned her coat, for the beer was making her sweat. And then she smelled it: the sweetness of the blood that stained her dress. Her beautiful Bowery Girl dress, ruined. She saw the reds of the soaked rags, the white of the muslin, the black of Annabelle's eyes, surprised and afraid.

"Damn airs you got now," Seamus said.

"Why?'Cause I ain't sitting with you?"

"' Cause you're sitting with *her*. Should've burned down that charity place the first time you girls walked in. Saved us all a bunch of grief. Right, Tommy? Right?"

"Get out of here." Tommy tapped his index finger on the table and glared at Emmeline.

"They was invited same as you," Mollie said.

"Get out."

Emmeline DuPre merely sat and stared back.

"You have no right to be here," Tommy said. "No right."

"Don't talk to Miss DuPre like that." Charlie stood; his hands shook near his sides.

"Fucking lily-ass."

"Shut up, Tommy."

"You're all what make this neighborhood so bad," Charlie said.

"We are, are we?" Hugh pushed his chair back, then smacked the top of his bowler to set it tighter on his head. "What the hell you know about anything, you little lily-ass?"

"Oh, good, let's fight," Mollie said. "What a surprise." She pulled her hand from under Emmeline's and stepped over to the Growlers' table and tore a glass from Seamus's grasp. Holding it high, she said, "Goddamn the Fourth Ward. Goddamn you, Tommy. And you, Seamus. Goddamn Mugs and Hugh. Goddamn all of us for not caring there weren't no railings on the stairs. Goddamn Annabelle for dying. And goddamn me for not being able to stop her."

She tossed back the drink. The room pulsated with silence. "Doesn't no one know 'Annabel Lee'? She used to sing it to me. Jesus, don't no one know the song? She loved that damn song."

CHOPIN

MOLLIE FOUND HERSELF ALONE in the clean white of the settlement house vestibule. There was only the swish of her new skirt, the surprise of catching her reflection in the smooth glass. The material of the skirt was a solid, indifferent brown. The spot of lace that showed above her black coat was coarse. It was what she could afford.

The gaslights to the interior rooms had been extinguished, the shades drawn on the windows facing the yard. The hallway door that led to the classes was open; from beyond, there came one solitary note of a piano. Then another, higher. A pause. Then notes played softly, like sighs, followed by spaces of emptiness or longing. The notes played around Mollie like an embrace, pulling her toward the door.

She stepped into the hallway and spied the flush of candlelight from the library. The door was slightly ajar. She peered in at the shelves of used books, the framed picture of President Chester A. Arthur staring gallantly past his glorious side-whiskers, the vase of peach roses. She pushed against the door to see farther. Miss DuPre sat at the upright piano; she hummed quietly what her hands played.

The music coated the air; Mollie stepped into it, felt it surround her. She had heard nothing so beautiful in her life.

The notes stopped, sudden enough that Mollie was sure she could see them float, then fall like petals against the rug. The piano stool squeaked as Emmeline turned around.

"In general, doors are meant to be knocked upon."

"It's just, the music, it was—"

"Chopin."

"It was beautiful. Not all clangy like dancehall stuff. Not that I don't like dancehall music."

Miss DuPre reached to the piano's top, and took down a cigarette and a match. She dragged the match across the bottom of her shoe, held the flame to the tobacco, and inhaled.

"I've come to say good-bye."

There was a rustle of fabric as Emmeline crossed one leg over the other. Smoking, an elbow on her knee, she didn't look much different from the streetwalkers who came to rest at Lefty's. But her skin was smooth and her eyes curious, instead of halfway dead like the girls on the street. "Are you going to Brooklyn?"

"Yes."

"I see."

"How come you ain't married?"

"Excuse me?"

"It's a little weird, ain't it, not to be married at your age? And living down here when you probably got everything in the world uptown. You don't even take a carriage, for Christ's sake. I don't see any rich people coming through here and patting people on the head like pets. That's what they used to do at the orphanage. You don't preach to us about God and repentance."

"I don't feel there's any need to repent. I feel life is lived by looking forward. By doing one good thing each day. That's enough, isn't it?"

"Annabelle says something like that. She's got a lot of sayings. *Had* a lot of sayings."

"Mmm." Emmeline lifted an eyebrow. "What lures you to Brooklyn?"

"I promised Annabelle we'd go."

"And will it be better there than here?"

"I want to be good."

"You already are good."

"I want to move to Brooklyn and meet nice people and not give a thought about picking their pockets. I want to walk down the street without turning my head all the time wondering if a cop's on my tail. I want someone to come pick up the dead horse that's been at the end of my block for two weeks. I want to walk into a café and not have the waiter make me prove I've got the money. I wanted that baby to have a better life than me and Annabelle had." She put her head in her hands, then, and let the sobs shake her chest. "I don't know what to do but that. I loved her." Her lungs burned, her throat was raw, and she could not stop crying. She clenched her teeth and dug her fingers into her ribcage, trying to stop crying. She knew tears brought nothing but more tears.

Emmeline did not move toward her, but finished her cigarette and slowly ground it out in the glass ashtray atop the piano.

Finally, Mollie was able to draw in one clean breath. Then another. Enough then to lift her head. "You never answered me."

"About what?"

"Why you came back here."

"I'm sick of the dead horse, too. And the poverty. The lack of education. The inability of people to see they are more than the Ward. That is why I came back."

"But the horse is still there and people is still poor."

"One small thing at a time."

"You got a lot of money. Maybe you'd be better off giving twenty dollars to every person you meet. They'd know what to do with it, maybe better than you."

"If I had given you twenty dollars the day before you walked into the settlement house, what would you have done with the money?"

"Paid the rent."

"Why don't you stay here and continue your typing? I could make a room for you. It could be the first dormitory room."

"I wanna go to Brooklyn. Me and Annabelle been dreaming of Brooklyn so long."

"I've found that the place you live doesn't matter," Emmeline said. "But *how* you live in that place does. Stay here. Don't squander opportunity."

"Squander it? I'm taking it. That's the new life I been planning for. How come you can't see that?"

Emmeline sighed. "When are you going?"

"Opening day."

"You don't need my blessing to cross that bridge, Miss Flynn."

"Did I ask for that?"

"In your way." Emmeline stood, and reached in her pocket. She then grasped Mollie's hand and held it tight. "Good luck to you, Mollie Flynn."

She left twenty dollars in Mollie's palm.

OPENING DAY,

May 24, 1883

HOW PEOPLE JOSTLED AND pushed! Ladies with parasols meant to block the sun were shouted at for blocking the view. A man in a gray morning suit had his top hat whisked from his head and crushed, just because he had stopped for a breath on the long stretch between New York and Brooklyn. Mollie felt fingers poking her ribs, urging her forward. But she grabbed the huge gray railing and clung tight.

The sun beat full on her skin. It was a fine day; a goddamn beautiful blue sky. She was here, smack in the middle of the bridge between two vast cities, between their great buildings of brick and granite. The river below reflected the reds, whites, and blues of the flags that festooned the man-o'wars and ferries and clippers. All the buildings along the East River bore flags, all the windows and rooftops and streets were full to bursting with the grays and blacks and browns of people come to see President Arthur and Governor Grover Cleveland cross the bridge to shake hands with the mayor of Brooklyn. Of course , the bridge was too vast for anyone to witness this; but many would go home and remember the day as if they *had* seen the regiment march by, *had* walked close behind the president and governor, and some might even remember receiving a smile or nod meant just for them.

Mollie Flynn cared nothing for the pomp and circumstance that began the day. What mattered to her was this moment now: crossing the bridge to Brooklyn, just as she promised Annabelle they would do. Slung across her shoulder was a small satchel; she put her hand inside to assure herself nothing had been stolen. Not that there was anything worthwhile for a pickpocket to steal. Just a broken piece of mirror, the small containers of Annabelle's paints, the trinket box that held one piece of paper: *Hapy Berthday—from me.* Nothing else.

She had promised Annabelle they would cross the bridge together and gain new lives, and though she could not take Annabelle, she could at least take her things.

Mollie remained midway between the two cities, one hand holding a railing that still smelled of paint.

Was it true, once a person passed the rough docks and warehouses, that the sky was bluer in Brooklyn? That there was space and light and rolling hills and cows? She and Annabelle had never gone to Brooklyn to find out.

Everything the girls learned had been gathered by watching the stereoscopes in the dime museum and reading newspapers glued to the walls of home. Not once had they taken a ferry over to see.

All they thought was: It's better than where we are.

And yet—and this is what kept Mollie Flynn's hand

tethered to the railing—it was possible it would be no different than the city she came from. There would still be sailors and saloons and dancehalls, and boys like the Growlers, and the room she could afford alone might be smaller than the one she had left.

She felt the warmth of a man standing next to her. He ate a ham sandwich and dusted the crumbs from his linen jacket. He glanced down at her, taking in her cheap Bowery dress.

"Eighth Wonder of the World." He held out his straw bowler. "Give a tip to the cities."

"Yer half-drunk."

"Just been toasting both towns."

She set the hat on her head for a brief second, then tipped it to the unknown of Brooklyn. She turned then to the docks and streets she knew like the back of her hand. She doffed the hat to the buntings and flags and ships.

"Thanks." She handed back the bowler to the doubly drunk gentleman and stepped past him.

Which way? Turn left, turn right.

Emmeline Dupre had entrusted twenty dollars to her, to do with as she pleased.

If I had given you twenty dollars the day before you walked into the settlement house, what would you have done with the money?

Mollie smiled. Asked someone to pick up the horse. Put a railing on the stairs to home, so no other Annabelle Lee would die from having nothing to stop her fall. She held her hand over the watch Annabelle had given her, feeling the regular beat of it against her chest.

She checked the time—3:45 P.M.—then stepped into the crowds and turned toward home.

Author's Note

THIS NOVEL BEGAN WITH the chance purchase of a single book at a dusty used-bookstore. The book, *How the Other Half Lives*, was author and photographer Jacob Riis's eye-opening study of tenement life in late nineteenth-century New York. Within its pages, Riis chronicles the poverty and despair and grit of the people who inhabited the slums. Here are the gamblers and thieves and immigrants. Here are the twenty thousand "street Arabs"—children turned out from home by families unable to afford them. Here are the tanneries and stale-beer dives, Blindman's Alley, and the notorious tenement Gotham Court.

I was awed, at first, by the sheer grimness reflected in the photos. But then I became awed by the sheer courage and tenacity of the people who tried to make their way within the narrow confines of the alleys and streets. And here began the story of the pickpocket Mollie Flynn and the prostitute Annabelle Lee, two young women who fended for themselves and had never known family or education.

Research for this novel included: *How the Other Half Lives* by Jacob Riis; *New York by Gaslight* by James D. McCabe, Jr., a wonderful 1882 tour of New York by carriage and ferry and elevated railway; *The Gangs of New York* by

Herbert Asbury; *Low Life* by Luc Sante; New York: *Sunshine and Shadow* by Roger Whitehouse (with excellent photographs of all the boroughs and classes of New York between 1860 and 1915); *Old New York in Early Photographs 1853-1901*, from the Collection of the New-York Historical Society, by Mary Black; *Sins of New York*, a compilation of articles from the Police Gazette; *Cheap Amusements: Working Women and Leisure in Turn-of-the-Century New York* by Kathy Peiss; *The City in Slang* by Irving Lewis Allen; *Incredible New York* by Lloyd Morris; *The Virtues of the Vicious* by Keith Gandal; and *Tales of Gaslight New York* compiled by Frank Oppel. Settlement house history included *A Useful Woman: The Early Life of Jane Addams* by Gioia Diliberto. Maps of the tenements (including stories, occupants, evidence of cholera or smallpox, and outhouses per person) came from the Peter C. Baldwin's incredible Web site: *The Fourth Ward: Life and Death in New York, 1860-1870.* More photos came from the Byron Collection at the Museum of the City of New York.

Bowery Girl is historical fiction in the sense that the world Mollie Flynn and Annabelle Lee inhabited cannot be traced on the modern streets of Manhattan. The tenements and rear rookeries have been razed or at least improved. Castle Garden, the Rat Pit, Batavia, and Oak Street are gone. The Brooklyn Bridge is no longer commonly considered one of the great wonders of the world.

To research 1883 Manhattan is to conjure ghosts, to dig through contemporary and historical accounts that sometimes glorify and exaggerate both rich and poor, both goodness and evil. The specifics in research, beyond dates and places and streets, came from studying the photographs of the time—exploring the dimness of the gaslights, the children playing in a street and blithely unaware of the dead horse lying ten feet away, the thick layer of grease on a tenement wall, a momentary smile.

Walking, for a moment, with two young women who want only a bit of sunshine and a chance for something better.

Mollie Flynn and Annabelle Lee can still be found: on the streets of Mumbai or Mexico City, down an alley in Detroit or Cleveland. Around the corner. This is not a novel about pain or poverty. It is a story of friendship and survival, and the ability to dream in the midst of insurmountable odds.

Acknowledgments

BOOKS ARE MADE BY many hands—I wish to thank those who helped in this one: George Nicholson, for creative guidance during many early drafts, and for his incredible support; Sharyn November for incisive editing, awesome ideas, and just being passionate about books and teens in general; Regina Hayes for believing in the story; Eileen Morales and Melanie Bower from the Museum of the City of New York for providing me an opportunity to view the original Jacob Riis lantern slides; and the Tenement Museum for giving us an incredible chance to experience the history and lives of those who once inhabited the Bowery and Lower East Side. Thank you also to Nina Solomita, a great friend, who has been there every step of the way, from concept to plot to paragraph to sentence to semicolon; my mother, Brigitte Leyde, for insisting I believe in myself and how I live in the world; and my father, Gary Taylor, for providing me the space in which to write this book, and whose love of books and words I so happily share. And finally, to Dana Blakemore, who is my everything.

About the Author

MY MISSION is to write historical fiction and romance that explores women's lives and brings their struggles and triumphs out of the shadows of history and onto the canvas of our American past. I wish to share the stories of women whose lives are untold, who don't exist in textbooks: the disenfranchised, the forgotten, those with double lives and huge hearts filled with weakness and courage.

My current novel, **Under the Pale Moon**, is due for release in 2015. Set in post-World War II Monterey, California, it explores the relationship of a married woman breaking the bonds of conformity, and a combat nurse haunted by the ghosts of war.

My interactive historical romances **The Very Thought of You** and **It Don't Mean a Thing**, are out now on Kindle and SilkWords.com. I am also the author of **Cissy Funk**, winner of the WILLA Literary Award for Best Young Adult Fiction.

Sign up at the link below to receive information on future releases.

http://eepurl.com/2CzHj

You can reach me at www.kimtaylorblakemore.com.

I love to hear from readers and would be very appreciative if you would consider writing a review on Amazon or GoodReads!